Aesop's Fables

(*Illustrated*)

A New Revised Version from Original Sources

by
Aesop

Illustrated by

HARRISON WEIR, JOHN TENNIEL, ERNEST GRISET

AND OTHERS

Petra Books

www.PetraBooks.com

Aesop's Fables (Illustrated)

Contents

Æsop's Fables

A NEW REVISED VERSION

FROM ORIGINAL SOURCES

WITH UPWARDS OF 200 ILLUSTRATIONS

BY

HARRISON WEIR, JOHN TENNIEL, ERNEST GRISET

AND OTHERS

NEW YORK
FRANK F. LOVELL & COMPANY
142 and 144 Worth Street

Aesop's Fables (Illustrated)

LIFE OF ÆSOP

The Life and History of Æsop is involved, like that of Homer, the most famous of Greek poets, in much obscurity. Sardis, the capital of Lydia; Samos, a Greek island; Mesembria, an ancient colony in Thrace; and Cotiæum, the chief city of a province of Phrygia, contend for the distinction of being the birthplace of Æsop. Although the honor thus claimed cannot be definitely assigned to any one of these places, yet there are a few incidents now generally accepted by scholars as established facts, relating to the birth, life, and death of Æsop. He is, by an almost universal consent, allowed to have been born about the year 620 B.C., and to have been by birth a slave. He was owned by two masters in succession, both inhabitants of Samos, Xanthus and Jadmon, the latter of whom gave him his liberty as a reward for his learning and wit. One of the privileges of a freedman in the ancient republics of Greece was the permission to take an active interest in public affairs; and Æsop, like the philosophers Phædo, Menippus, and Epictetus, in later times, raised himself from the indignity of a servile condition to a position of high renown. In his desire alike to instruct and to be instructed, he travelled through many countries, and among others came to Sardis, the capital of the famous king of Lydia, the great patron in that day, of learning and of learned men. He met at the court of Crœsus with Solon, Thales, and other sages, and is related so to have pleased his royal master, by the part he took in the conversations held with these philosophers, that he applied to him an expression which has since passed into a proverb, "μᾶλλον ὁ Φρύξ"— "The Phrygian has spoken better than all."

On the invitation of Crœsus he fixed his residence at Sardis, and was employed by that monarch in various difficult and delicate affairs of state. In his discharge of these commissions he visited the different petty republics of Greece. At one time he is found in Corinth, and at another in Athens, endeavoring, by the narration of some of his wise fables, to reconcile the inhabitants of those cities to the administration of their respective rulers, Pariander and Pisistratus. One of these ambassadorial missions, undertaken at the command of Crœsus, was the occasion of his death. Having been sent to Delphi with a large sum of gold for distribution among the citizens, he was so provoked at their covetousness that he refused to divide the money, and sent it back to his master. The Delphians, enraged at this treatment, accused him of impiety, and, in spite of his sacred character as ambassador, executed him as a public criminal. This cruel death of Æsop was not unavenged. The citizens of Delphi were visited with a series of calamities, until they made a public reparation of their crime; and "The blood of Æsop" became a well-known adage, bearing witness to the truth that deeds of wrong would not pass unpunished. Neither did the great fabulist lack posthumous honors; for a statue was erected to his memory at Athens, the work of Lysippus, one of the most famous of Greek sculptors. Phædrus thus immortalizes the event:—

Æsopo ingentem statuam posuere Attici,
Servumque collocarunt æterna in basi:
Patere honoris scirent ut cuncti viam;
Nec generi tribui sed virtuti gloriam.

These few facts are all that can be relied on with any degree of certainty, in reference to the birth, life, and death of Æsop. They were first brought to light, after a patient search and diligent perusal of ancient authors, by a Frenchman, M. Claude Gaspard Bachet de Mezeriac, who declined the honor of being tutor to Louis XIII. of France, from his desire to devote himself exclusively to literature. He published his life of Æsop, Anno Domini 1632. The later investigations of a host of English and German scholars have added very little to the facts given by M. Mezeriac. The substantial truth of his statements has been confirmed by later criticism and inquiry.

It remains to state, that prior to this publication of M. Mezeriac, the life of Æsop was from the pen of Maximus Planudes, a monk of Constantinople, who was sent on an embassy to Venice by the Byzantine Emperor Andronicus the elder, and who wrote in the early part of the fourteenth century. His life was prefixed to all the early editions of these fables, and was republished as late as 1727 by Archdeacon Croxall as the introduction to his edition of Æsop. This life by Planudes contains, however, so small an amount of truth, and is so full of absurd pictures of the grotesque deformity of Æsop, of wondrous apocryphal stories, of lying legends, and gross anachronisms, that it is now universally condemned as false, puerile, and unauthentic. It is given up in the present day, by general consent, as unworthy of the slightest credit.

Aesop's Fables (Illustrated)

The Wolf Turned Shepherd

A wolf, finding that the sheep were so afraid of him that he could not get near them, disguised himself in the dress of a shepherd, and thus attired approached the flock. As he came near, he found the shepherd fast asleep. As the sheep did not run away, he resolved to imitate the

voice of the shepherd. In trying to do so, he only howled, and awoke the shepherd. As he could not run away, he was soon killed.

Those who attempt to act in disguise are apt to overdo it.

The Stag at the Pool

A stag saw his shadow reflected in the water, and greatly admired the size of his horns, but felt angry with himself for having such weak feet. While he was thus contemplating himself, a Lion appeared at the pool. The Stag betook himself to flight, and kept himself with ease at a safe distance from the Lion, until he entered a wood and became entangled with his horns. The Lion quickly came up with him and caught him. When too late he thus reproached himself: "Woe is me! How have I deceived myself! These feet which would have saved me I despised, and I gloried in these antlers which have proved my destruction."

What is most truly valuable is often underrated.

The Fox and the Mask

A fox entered the house of an actor, and, rummaging through all his properties, came upon a Mask, an admirable imitation of a human head. He placed his paws on it, and said: "What a beautiful head! yet it is of no value, as it entirely wants brains."

A fair face is of little use without sense.

The Bear and the Fox

A bear boasted very much of his philanthropy, saying "that of all animals he was the most tender in his regard for man, for he had such respect for him, that he would not even touch his dead body." A Fox hearing these words said with a smile to the Bear: "Oh, that you would eat the dead and not the living!"

We should not wait till a person is dead, to give him our respect.

The Wolf and the Lamb

A Wolf, meeting with a Lamb astray from the fold, resolved not to lay violent hands on him, but to find some plea, which should justify to the Lamb himself his right to eat him. He then addressed him: "Sirrah, last year you grossly insulted me." "Indeed," bleated the Lamb in a mournful tone of voice, "I was not then born." Then said the Wolf: "You feed in my pasture." "No, good sir," replied the Lamb, "I have not yet tasted grass." Again said the Wolf: "You drink of my well." "No,"

exclaimed the Lamb, "I never yet drank water, for as yet my mother's milk is both food and drink to me." On which the Wolf seized him, and ate him up, saying: "Well! I won't remain supperless, even though you refute every one of my imputations."

The tyrant will always find a pretext for his tyranny, and it is useless for the innocent to try by reasoning to get justice, when the oppressor intends to be unjust.

The One-Eyed Doe

A Doe, blind of an eye, was accustomed to graze as near to the edge of the sea as she possibly could, to secure greater safety. She turned her eye towards the land, that she might perceive the approach of a hunter or hound, and her injured eye towards the sea, from which she entertained no anticipation of danger. Some boatmen, sailing by, saw her, and, taking a successful aim, mortally wounded her. Said she: "O wretched creature that I am! to take such precaution against the land, and, after all, to find this seashore, to which I had come for safety, so much more perilous."

Danger sometimes comes from a source that is least suspected.

The Dog, Cock and Fox

A Dog and a Cock, traveling together, took shelter at night in a thick wood. The Cock perched himself on a high branch, while the Dog found a bed at the foot of the tree. When morning dawned, the Cock, as usual, crowed very loudly. A Fox, hearing the sound, and wishing to make a breakfast on him, came and stood under the branches, saying how earnestly he desired to make the acquaintance of the owner of so sweet a voice.

"If you will admit me," said he, "I should very much like to spend the day with you."

The Cock said: "Sir, do me the favor to go round and wake up my porter, that he may open the door, and let you in." On the Fox approaching the tree, the Dog sprang out and caught him and quickly tore him in pieces.

Those who try to entrap others are often caught by their own schemes.

The Mouse, the Frog, and the Hawk

A Mouse, by an unlucky chance, formed an intimate acquaintance with a Frog. The Frog one day, intent on mischief, bound the foot of the Mouse tightly to his own. Thus joined together, the Frog led his friend toward the pool in which he lived, until he reached the very brink, when suddenly jumping in, he dragged the Mouse in with him. The Frog enjoyed the water amazingly, and swam croaking about as if he had done a meritorious action. The unhappy Mouse was soon suffocated with the water, and his dead body floated about on the surface, tied to the foot of the Frog. A Hawk observed it, and, pouncing upon it, carried it up aloft. The Frog, being still fastened to the leg of the Mouse, was also carried off a prisoner, and was eaten by the Hawk.

Harm hatch, harm catch.

The Dog and the Oyster

A Dog, used to eating eggs, saw an Oyster, and opening his mouth to its widest extent, swallowed it down with the utmost relish, supposing it to be an egg. Soon afterwards suffering great pain in his stomach, he said: "I deserve all this torment, for my folly in thinking that everything round must be an egg."

Who acts in haste repents at leisure.

The Wolf and the Shepherds

A Wolf passing by, saw some shepherds in a hut eating for their dinner a haunch of mutton. Approaching them, he said: "What a clamor you would raise, if I were to do as you are doing!"

Men are too apt to condemn in others the very things they practice themselves.

The Hares and the Frogs

The Hares, oppressed with a sense of their own exceeding timidity, and weary of the perpetual alarm to which they were exposed, with one accord determined to put an end to themselves and their troubles, by jumping from a lofty precipice into a deep lake below. As they scampered off in a very numerous body to carry out their resolve, the Frogs lying on the banks of the lake heard the noise of their feet, and rushed helter-skelter to the deep water for safety. On seeing the rapid disappearance of the Frogs, one of the Hares cried out to his companions: "Stay, my friends, do not do as you intended; for you now see that other creatures who yet live are more timorous than ourselves."

We are encouraged by seeing others that are worse off than ourselves.

The Lion and the Boar

On a summer day, when the great heat induced a general thirst, a Lion and a Boar came at the same moment to a small well to drink. They fiercely disputed which of them should drink first, and were soon engaged in the agonies of a mortal combat. On their stopping on a sudden to take breath for the fiercer renewal of the strife, they saw some Vultures waiting in the distance to feast on the one which should fall first. They at once made up their quarrel, saying: "It is better for us to make friends, than to become the food of Crows or Vultures, as will certainly happen if we are disabled."

Those who strive are often watched by others who will take advantage of their defeat to benefit themselves.

The Mischievous Dog

A Dog used to run up quietly to the heels of those he met, and to bite them without notice. His master sometimes suspended a bell about his neck, that he might give notice of his presence wherever he went, and sometimes he fastened a chain about his neck, to which was attached a heavy clog, so that he could not be so quick at biting people's heels.

The Dog grew proud of his bell and clog, and went with them all over the market-place. An old hound said to him: "Why do you make such an exhibition of yourself? That bell and clog that you carry are not, believe me, orders of merit, but, on the contrary, marks of disgrace, a public notice to all men to avoid you as an ill-mannered dog."

Those who achieve notoriety often mistake it for fame.

The Quack Frog

A Frog once made proclamation to all the beasts that he was a learned physician, and able to heal all diseases. A Fox asked him: "How can you pretend to prescribe for others, and you are unable to heal your own lame gait and wrinkled skin?"

Those who pretend that they can mend others should first mend themselves, and then they will be more readily believed.

The Ass, the Fox, and the Lion

The Ass and the Fox, having entered into a partnership together, went out into the forest to hunt. They had not proceeded far, when they met a Lion. The Fox approached the Lion and promised to contrive for him the capture of the Ass, if he would pledge his word that his own life should be spared. On his assuring him that he would not injure him, the Fox led the Ass to a deep pit, and contrived that he should fall into it. The Lion, seeing that the Ass was secured, immediately clutched the Fox, and then attacked the Ass at his leisure.

Traitors must expect treachery.

The Wolf and the Sheep

A Wolf, being sick and maimed, called to a Sheep, who was passing, and asked him to fetch some water from the stream. "For," he said, "if you will bring me drink, I will find means to provide myself with meat." "Yes," said the Sheep, "if I should bring you the draught, you would doubtless make me provide the meat also."

Hypocritical speeches are easily seen through.

The Cock and the Jewel

A Cock, scratching for food for himself and his hens, found a precious stone; on which he said: "If thy owner had found thee, and not I, he would have taken thee up, and have set thee in thy first estate; but I have found thee for no purpose.

I would rather have one barleycorn than all the jewels in the world.

The Two Pots

A river carried down in its stream two Pots, one made of earthenware, and the other of brass. As they floated along on the surface of the stream, the Earthen Pot said to the Brass Pot: "Pray keep at a distance, and do not come near me, for if you touch me ever so slightly, I shall be broken in pieces; and besides, I by no means wish to come near you.".

Equals make the best friends.

The Gnat and the Lion

A Gnat came and said to a Lion: "I do not the least fear you, nor are you stronger than I am. For in what does your strength consist? You can scratch with your claws, and bite with your teeth—so can a woman in her quarrels. I repeat that I am altogether more powerful than you; and if you doubt it, let us fight and see who will conquer." The Gnat, having sounded his horn, fastened itself upon the Lion, and stung him on the nostrils. The Lion, trying to crush him, tore himself with his claws, until he punished himself severely. The Gnat thus prevailed over the Lion, and buzzing about in a song of triumph, flew away. But shortly afterwards he became entangled in the meshes of a cobweb, and was eaten by a spider. He greatly lamented his fate, saying: "Woe is me, that I, who can wage war successfully with the hugest beasts, should perish myself from this spider."

The Widow and her Little Maidens

A widow woman, fond of cleaning, had two little maidens to wait on her. She was in the habit of waking them early in the morning, at cockcrow. The maidens, being aggrieved by such excessive labor, resolved to kill the cock who roused their mistress so early. When they had done this, they found that they had only prepared for themselves greater troubles, for their mistress, no longer hearing the cock, was unable to tell the time, and so, woke them up to their work in the middle of the night.

Unlawful acts to escape trials only increase our troubles.

The Fox and the Lion

A Fox who had never yet seen a Lion, when he fell in with him by a certain chance for the first time in the forest, was so frightened that he was near dying with fear. On his meeting with him for the second time, he was still much alarmed, but not to the same extent as at first. On seeing him the third time, he so increased in boldness that he went up to him, and commenced a familiar conversation with him.

Acquaintance softens prejudices.

The Boy and the Nettle

A Boy was stung by a Nettle. He ran home and told his mother, saying: "Although it pains me so much, I did but touch it ever so gently." "That was just it," said his mother, "which caused it to sting you. The next time you touch a Nettle, grasp it boldly, and it will be soft as silk to your hand, and not in the least hurt you."

Whatever you do, do with all your might.

The Monkey and the Dolphin

A Sailor, bound on a long voyage, took with him a Monkey to amuse him while on shipboard. As he sailed off the coast of Greece, a violent tempest arose, in which the ship was wrecked, and he, his Monkey and all the crew were obliged to swim for their lives. A Dolphin saw the Monkey contending with the waves, and supposing him to be a man (whom he is always said to befriend), came and placed himself under him, to convey him on his back in safety to the shore. When the Dolphin arrived with his burden in sight of land not far from Athens, he demanded of the Monkey if he were an Athenian, who answered that he was, and that he was descended from one of the noblest families in that city.

The Dolphin then inquired if he knew the Piræus (the famous harbor of Athens). The Monkey, supposing that a man was meant, and being obliged to support his previous lie, answered that he knew him very well, and that he was an intimate friend, who would, no doubt, be very glad to see him. The Dolphin, indignant at these falsehoods, dipped the Monkey under the water, and drowned him.

He who once begins to tell falsehoods is obliged to tell others to make them appear true, and, sooner or later, they will get him into trouble.

The Game-cocks and the Partridge

A Man had two Game-cocks in his poultry yard. One day, by chance, he fell in with a tame Partridge for sale. He purchased it, and brought it home that it might be reared with his Game-cocks. On its being put into the poultry-yard, they struck at it, and followed it about, so that the Partridge was grievously troubled in mind, and supposed that he was thus badly treated because he was a stranger. Not long afterwards he saw the Cocks fighting together, and not separating before one had well beaten the other. He then said to himself: "I shall no longer distress myself at being struck at by these Game-cocks, when I see that they cannot even refrain from quarreling with each other."

Strangers should avoid those who quarrel among themselves.

The Town Mouse and the Country Mouse

A Country Mouse invited a Town Mouse, an intimate friend, to pay him a visit, and partake of his country fare. As they were on the bare plough-lands, eating their wheat-stalks and roots pulled up from the hedge-row, the Town Mouse said to his friend: "You live here the life of the ants, while in my house is the horn of plenty. I am surrounded with every luxury, and if you will come with me, as I much wish you would, you shall have an ample share of my dainties." The Country Mouse was easily persuaded, and returned to town with his friend. On his arrival, the Town Mouse placed before him bread, barley, beans, dried figs, honey, raisins, and, last of all, brought a dainty piece of cheese from a basket. The Country Mouse, being much delighted at the sight of such good cheer, expressed his satisfaction in warm terms, and lamented his own hard fate. Just as they were beginning to eat, some one opened the door, and they both ran off squeaking, as fast as they could, to a hole so narrow that two could only find room in it by squeezing. They had scarcely again begun their repast when some one else entered to take something out of a cupboard, on which the two Mice, more frightened than before, ran away and hid themselves. At last the Country Mouse, almost famished, thus addressed his friend: "Although you have prepared for me so dainty a feast, I must leave you to enjoy it by yourself. It is surrounded by too many dangers to please me."

Better a little in safety, than an abundance surrounded by danger.

The Trumpeter taken Prisoner

A Trumpeter, bravely leading on the soldiers, was captured by the enemy. He cried out to his captors: "Pray spare me, and do not take my life without cause or without injury. I have not slain a single man of your troop. I have no arms, and carry nothing but this one brass trumpet." "That is the very reason for which you should be put to death," they said, "for while you do not fight yourself, your loud trumpet stirs up all the other soldiers to battle."

He who incites strife is as guilty as they who strive.

The Fatal Marriage

The Lion, touched with gratitude by the noble procedure of a Mouse, and resolving not to be outdone in generosity by any wild beast whatsoever, desired his little deliverer to name his own terms, for that he might depend upon his complying with any proposal he should make. The Mouse, fired with ambition at this gracious offer, did not so much consider what was proper for him to ask, as what was in the powers of his prince to grant; and so demanded his princely daughter, the young lioness, in marriage. The Lion consented; but, when he would have given the royal virgin into his possession, she, like a giddy thing as she was, not minding how she walked, by chance set her paw upon her spouse, who was coming to meet her, and crushed him to pieces.

Beware of unequal matches. Alliances prompted by ambition often prove fatal.

The Ass and the Charger

An Ass congratulated a Horse on being so ungrudgingly and carefully provided for, while he himself had scarcely enough to eat, nor even that without hard work. But when war broke out, the heavy armed soldier mounted the Horse, and rushed into the very midst of the enemy, and the Horse, being wounded, fell dead on the battle-field. Then the Ass, seeing all these things, changed his mind, and commiserated the Horse, saying: "How much more fortunate am I than a charger. I can remain at home in safety while he is exposed to all the perils of war."

Be not hasty to envy the condition of others.

The Vain Jackdaw

Jupiter determined, it is said, to create a sovereign over the birds, and made proclamation that, on a certain day, they should all present themselves before him, when he would himself choose the most beautiful among them to be king. The Jackdaw, knowing his own ugliness, searched through the woods and fields, and collected the feathers which had fallen from the wings of his companions, and stuck them in all parts of his

body. When the appointed day arrived, and the birds had assembled before Jupiter, the Jackdaw also made his appearance in his many-feathered finery. On Jupiter proposing to make him king, on account of the beauty of his plumage, the birds indignantly protested, and each plucking from him his own feathers, the Jackdaw was again nothing but a Jackdaw.

Hope not to succeed in borrowed plumes.

The Milkmaid and her Pot of Milk

A Maid was carrying her pail of milk to the farm-house, when she fell a-musing. "The money for which this milk will be sold will buy at least three hundred eggs. The eggs, allowing for all mishaps, will produce two hundred and fifty chickens. The chickens will become ready for market when poultry will fetch the highest price; so that by the end of the year I shall have money enough to buy a new gown. In this dress I will go to the Christmas junketings, when all the young fellows will propose to me, but I will toss my head, and refuse them every one." At this moment she tossed her head in unison with her thoughts, when down fell the Milk-pot to the ground, and broke into a hundred pieces, and all her fine schemes perished in a moment.

Count not your chickens before they are hatched.

The Playful Ass

An Ass climbed up to the roof of a building, and, frisking about there, broke in the tiling. The owner went up after him, and quickly drove him down, beating him severely with a thick wooden cudgel. The Ass said: "Why, I saw the Monkey do this very thing yesterday, and you all laughed heartily, as if it afforded you very great amusement."

Those who do not know their right place must be taught it.

The Man and the Satyr

A Man and a Satyr once formed a bond of alliance. One very cold wintry day, as they talked together, the Man put his fingers to his mouth and blew on them. On the Satyr inquiring the reason, he told him that he did it to warm his hands. Later on in the day they sat down to eat, the food prepared being quite scalding. The Man raised one of his dishes towards his mouth and blew in it.

On the Satyr again inquiring the reason, he said that he did it to cool the meat. "I can no longer consider you as a friend," said the Satyr; "a fellow who with the same breath blows hot and cold I could never trust."

A man who talks for both sides is not to be trusted by either.

The Oak and the Reeds

A very large Oak was uprooted by the wind, and thrown across a stream. It fell among some Reeds, which it thus addressed: "I wonder how you, who are so light and weak, are not entirely crushed by these strong winds." They replied:

"You fight and contend with the wind, and consequently you are destroyed; while we, on the contrary, bend before the least breath of air, and therefore remain unbroken."

Stoop to conquer.

The Huntsman and the Fisherman

A Huntsman, returning with his dogs from the field, fell in by chance with a Fisherman, bringing home a basket laden with fish. The Huntsman wished to have the fish, and their owner experienced an equal longing for the contents of the game-bag. They quickly agreed to exchange the produce of their day's sport. Each was so well pleased with his bargain, that they made for some time the same exchange day after day. A neighbor said to them: "If you go on in this way, you will soon destroy, by frequent use, the pleasure of your exchange, and each will again wish to retain the fruits of his own sport."

Pleasures are heightened by abstinence.

The Mother and the Wolf

A famished Wolf was prowling about in the morning in search of food. As he passed the door of a cottage built in the forest, he heard a mother say to her child: "Be quiet, or I will throw you out of the window, and the Wolf shall eat you." The Wolf sat all day waiting at the door. In the evening he heard the same woman fondling her child, and saying: "He is quiet now, and if the Wolf should come, we will kill him." The Wolf, hearing these words, went home, gaping with cold and hunger.

Be not in haste to believe what is said in anger or thoughtlessness.

The Shepherd and the Wolf

A Shepherd once found a young Wolf, and brought it up, and after a while taught it to steal lambs from the neighboring flocks. The Wolf, having shown himself an apt pupil, said to the Shepherd: "Since you have taught me to steal, you must keep a sharp look-out, or you will lose some of your own flock."

The vices we teach may be practiced against us.

The Dove and the Crow

A Dove shut up in a cage was boasting of the large number of the young ones which she had hatched. A Crow, hearing her, said: "My good friend, cease from this unreasonable boasting. The larger the number of your family, the greater your cause of sorrow, in seeing them shut up in this prison-house."

To enjoy our blessings we must have freedom.

The Old Man and the Three Young Men

As an old man was planting a tree, three young men came along and began to make sport of him, saying: "It shows your foolishness to be planting a tree at your age. The tree cannot bear fruit for many years, while you must very soon die. What is the use of your wasting your time in providing pleasure for others

to share long after you are dead?" The old man stopped in his labor and replied: "Others before me provided for my happiness, and it is my duty to provide for those who shall come after me. As for life, who is sure of it for a day? You may all die before me." The old man's words came true; one of the young men went on a voyage at sea and was drowned, another went to war and was shot, and the third fell from a tree and broke his neck.

We should not think wholly of ourselves, and we should remember that life is uncertain.

The Lion and the Fox

A Fox entered into partnership with a Lion, on the pretense of becoming his servant. Each undertook his proper duty in accordance with his own nature and powers. The Fox discovered and pointed out the prey, the Lion sprang on it and seized it. The Fox soon became jealous of the Lion carrying off the Lion's share, and said that he would no longer find out the prey, but would capture it on his own account. The next day he attempted to snatch a lamb from the fold, but fell himself a prey to the huntsman and his hounds.

Keep to your place, if you would succeed.

The Horse and the Stag

The Horse had the plain entirely to himself. A Stag intruded into his domain and shared his pasture. The Horse, desiring to revenge himself on the stranger, requested a man, if he were willing, to help him in punishing the Stag. The man replied, that if the Horse would receive a bit in his mouth, and agree to carry him, he would contrive very effectual weapons against the Stag. The Horse consented, and allowed the man to mount him.

From that hour he found that, instead of obtaining revenge on the Stag, he had enslaved himself to the service of man.

He who seeks to injure others often injures only himself.

The Lion and the Dolphin

A Lion, roaming by the sea-shore, saw a Dolphin lift up its head out of the waves, and asked him to contract an alliance with him; saying that of all the animals, they ought to be the best friends, since the one was the king of beasts on the earth, and the other was the sovereign ruler of all the inhabitants of the ocean. The Dolphin gladly consented to this request. Not long afterwards the Lion had a combat with a wild bull, and called on the Dolphin to help him. The Dolphin, though quite willing to give him assistance, was unable to do so, as he could not by any means reach the land. The Lion abused him as a traitor. The Dolphin replied: "Nay, my friend, blame not me, but Nature, which, while giving me the sovereignty of the sea, has quite denied me the power of living upon the land."

Let every one stick to his own element.

The Mice in Council

The Mice summoned a council to decide how they might best devise means for obtaining notice of the approach of their great enemy the Cat. Among the many plans devised, the one that found most favor was the proposal to tie a bell to the neck of the Cat, that the Mice, being warned by the sound of the tinkling, might run away and hide themselves in their holes at his approach. But when the Mice further debated who among them should thus "bell the Cat," there was no one found to do it.

Let those who propose be willing to perform.

The Camel and the Arab

An Arab Camel-driver having completed the lading of his Camel, asked him which he would like best, to go up hill or down hill. The poor beast replied, not without a touch of reason: "Why do you ask me?

Is it that the level way through the desert is closed?"

The Fighting Cocks and the Eagle

Two Game Cocks were fiercely fighting for the mastery of the farm-yard. One at last put the other to flight. The vanquished Cock skulked away and hid himself in a quiet corner. The conqueror, flying up to a high wall, flapped his wings and crowed exultingly with all his might. An Eagle sailing through the air pounced upon him, and carried him off in his talons. The vanquished Cock immediately came out of his corner, and ruled henceforth with undisputed mastery.

Pride goes before destruction.

The Boys and the Frogs

Some boys, playing near a pond, saw a number of Frogs in the water, and began to pelt them with stones. They killed several of them, when one of the Frogs, lifting his head out of the water, cried out: "Pray stop, my boys; what is sport to you is death to us."

What we do in sport often makes great trouble for others.

The Crab and its Mother

A Crab said to her son: "Why do you walk so one-sided, my child? It is far more becoming to go straight forward." The young Crab replied: "Quite true, dear mother; and if you will show me the straight way, I will promise to walk in it." The mother tried in vain, and submitted without remonstrance to the reproof of her child.

Example is more powerful than precept.

The Wolf and the Shepherd

A Wolf followed a flock of sheep for a long time, and did not attempt to injure one of them. The Shepherd at first stood on his guard against him, as against an enemy, and kept a strict watch over his movements. But when the Wolf, day after day, kept in the company of the sheep, and did not make the slightest effort to seize them, the Shepherd began to look upon him as a guardian of his flock rather than as a plotter of evil against it; and when occasion called him one day into the city, he left the sheep entirely in his charge. The Wolf, now that he had the opportunity, fell upon the sheep, and destroyed the greater part of the flock. The Shepherd, on his return, finding his flock destroyed, exclaimed: "I have been rightly served; why did I trust my sheep to a Wolf?"

An evil mind will show in evil action, sooner or later.

The Man and the Lion

A Man and a Lion traveled together through the forest. They soon began to boast of their respective superiority to each other in strength and prowess. As they were disputing, they passed a statue, carved in stone, which represented "A Lion strangled by a Man." The traveler pointed to it and said: "See there! How strong we are, and how we prevail over even the king of beasts." The Lion replied: "This statue was made by one of you men. If we Lions knew how to erect statues, you would see the man placed under the paw of the Lion."

One story is good till another is told.

The Ox and the Frog

An Ox, drinking at a pool, trod on a brood of young frogs, and crushed one of them to death. The mother, coming up and missing one of her sons, inquired of his brothers what had become of him. "He is dead, dear mother; for just now a very huge beast with four great feet came to the pool, and crushed him to death with his cloven heel." The Frog, puffing herself out, inquired, "If the beast was as big as that in size." "Cease, mother, to puff yourself out," said her son, "and do not be angry; for you would, I assure you, sooner burst than successfully imitate the hugeness of that monster."

Impossible things we cannot hope to attain, and it is of no use to try.

The Birds, the Beasts, and the Bat

The Birds waged war with the Beasts, and each party were by turns the conquerors. A Bat, fearing the uncertain issues of the fight, always betook himself to that side which was the strongest. When peace was proclaimed, his deceitful conduct was apparent to both the combatants; he was driven forth from the light of day, and henceforth concealed himself in dark hiding-places, flying always alone and at night.

Those who practice deceit must expect to be shunned.

The Charcoal-Burner and the Fuller

A Charcoal-burner carried on his trade in his own house. One day he met a friend, a Fuller, and entreated him to come and live with him, saying that they should be far better neighbors, and that their housekeeping expenses would be lessened. The Fuller replied: "The arrangement is impossible as far as I am concerned, for whatever I should whiten, you would immediately blacken again with your charcoal."

Like will draw like.

The Bull and the Goat

A Bull, escaping from a Lion, entered a cave, which some shepherds had lately occupied. A He-goat was left in it, who sharply attacked him with his horns. The Bull quietly addressed him—"Butt away as much as you will. I have no fear of you, but of the Lion. Let that monster once go, and I will soon let you know what is the respective strength of a Goat and a Bull."

It shows an evil disposition to take advantage of a friend in distress.

The Lion and the Mouse

A Lion was awakened from sleep by a Mouse running over his face. Rising up in anger, he caught him and was about to kill him, when the Mouse piteously entreated, saying: "If you would only spare my life, I would be sure to repay your kindness." The Lion laughed and let him go. It happened shortly after this that the Lion was caught by some hunters, who bound him by strong ropes to the ground. The Mouse, recognizing his roar, came up and gnawed the rope with his teeth, and, setting him free, exclaimed: "You ridiculed the idea of my ever being able to help you,

not expecting to receive from me any repayment of your favor; but now you know that it is possible for even a Mouse to confer benefits on a Lion."

No one is too weak to do good.

The Horse and the Ass

A Horse, proud of his fine trappings, met an Ass on the highway. The Ass being heavily laden moved slowly out of the way. "Hardly," said the Horse, "can I resist kicking you with my heels." The Ass held his peace, and made only a silent appeal to the justice of the gods. Not long afterward, the Horse, having become broken-winded, was sent by his owner to the farm. The Ass, seeing him drawing a dung-cart, thus derided him. "Where, O boaster, are now all thy gay trappings, thou who art thyself reduced to the condition you so lately treated with contempt?"

The Old Hound

A Hound, who in the days of his youth and strength had never yielded to any beast of the forest, encountered in his old age a boar in the chase. He seized him boldly by the ear, but could not retain his hold because of the decay of his teeth, so that the boar escaped. His master, quickly coming up, was very much disappointed, and fiercely abused the dog. The Hound looked up and said: "It was not my fault, master; my spirit was as good as ever, but I could not help mine infirmities. I rather deserve to be praised for what I have been, than to be blamed for what I am."

No one should be blamed for his infirmities.

The Crow and the Pitcher

A Crow, perishing with thirst, saw a pitcher, and, hoping to find water, flew to it with great delight. When he reached it, he discovered to his grief that it contained so little water that he could not possibly get at it. He tried everything he could think of to reach the water, but all his efforts were in vain. At last he collected as many stones as he could carry, and dropped them one by one with his beak into the pitcher, until he brought the water within his reach, and thus saved his life.

Necessity is the mother of invention.

The Ass Eating Thistles

An Ass was loaded with good provisions of several sorts, which, in time of harvest, he was carrying into the field for his master and the reapers to dine upon. By the way he met with a fine large Thistle, and, being very hungry, began to mumble it; and while he was doing so he entered into this reflection: "How many greedy epicures would think themselves happy, amidst such a variety of delicate viands as I now carry! But to me this bitter, prickly Thistle is more savory and relishing than the most exquisite and sumptuous banquet. Let others choose what they may for food, but give me, above everything, a fine juicy thistle like this and I will be content."

Every one to his taste: one man's meat is another man's poison, and one man's poison is another man's meat; what is rejected by one person may be valued very highly by another.

The Wolf and the Lion

A Wolf, having stolen a lamb from a fold, was carrying him off to his lair. A Lion met him in the path, and, seizing the lamb, took it from him. The Wolf, standing at a safe distance, exclaimed: "You have unrighteously taken from me that which was mine." The Lion jeeringly replied: "It was righteously yours, eh? Was it the gift of a friend, or did you get it by purchase? If you did not get it in one way or the other, how then did you come by it?"

One thief is no better than another.

The King's Son and the Painted Lion

A King who had one only son, fond of martial exercises, had a dream in which he was warned that his son would be killed by a lion. Afraid lest the dream should prove true, he built for his son a pleasant palace, and adorned its walls for his amusement with all kinds of animals of the size of life, among which was the picture of a lion. When the young Prince saw this, his grief at being thus confined burst out afresh, and standing near the lion, he thus spoke: "O you most detestable of animals! through a lying dream of my father's, which he saw in his sleep, I am shut up on your

account in this palace as if I had been a girl. What shall I now do to you?" With these words he stretched out his hands toward a thorn-tree, meaning to cut a stick from its branches that he might beat the lion, when one of its sharp prickles pierced his finger, and caused great pain and inflammation, so that the young Prince fell down in a fainting fit. A violent fever suddenly set in, from which he died not many days after.

We had better bear our troubles bravely than try to escape them.

The Trees and the Axe

A Man came into a forest, and made a petition to the Trees to provide him a handle for his axe. The Trees consented to his request, and gave him a young ash-tree. No sooner had the man fitted from it a new handle to his axe, than he began to use it, and quickly felled with his strokes the noblest giants of the forest. An old oak, lamenting when too late the destruction of his companions, said to a neighboring cedar: "The first step has lost us all. If we had not given up the rights of the ash, we might yet have retained our own privileges and have stood for ages."

In yielding the rights of others, we may endanger our own.

The Seaside Travelers

Some travelers, journeying along the sea-shore, climbed to the summit of a tall cliff, and from thence looking over the sea, saw in the distance what they thought was a large ship, and waited in the hope of seeing it enter the harbor. But as the object on which they looked was driven by the wind nearer to the shore, they found that it could at the most be a small boat, and not a ship. When, however, it reached the beach, they discovered that it was only a large fagot of sticks, and one of them said to his companions: "We have waited for no purpose, for after all there is nothing to see but a fagot."

Our mere anticipations of life outrun its realities.

The Sea-gull and the Kite

A Sea-gull, who was more at home swimming on the sea than walking on the land, was in the habit of catching live fish for its food. One day, having bolted down too large a fish, it burst its deep gullet-bag, and lay down on the shore to die. A Kite, seeing him, and thinking him a land bird like itself, exclaimed: "You richly deserve your fate; for a bird of the air has no business to seek its food from the sea."

Every man should be content to mind his own business.

The Monkey and the Camel

The beasts of the forest gave a splendid entertainment, at which the Monkey stood up and danced. Having vastly delighted the assembly, he sat down amidst universal applause. The Camel, envious of the praises bestowed on the Monkey, and desirous to divert to himself the favor of the guests, proposed to stand up in his turn, and dance for their amusement. He moved about in so very ridiculous a manner, that the Beasts, in a fit of indignation, set upon him with clubs, and drove him out of the assembly.

It is absurd to ape our betters.

The Rat and the Elephant

A Rat, traveling on the highway, met a huge elephant, bearing his royal master and his suite, and also his favorite cat and dog, and parrot and monkey. The great beast and his attendants were followed by an admiring crowd, taking up all of the road. "What fools you are," said the Rat to the people, "to make such a hubbub over an elephant. Is it his great bulk that you so much admire? It can only frighten little boys and girls, and I can do that as well. I am a beast; as well as he, and have as many legs and ears and eyes. He has no right to take up all the highway, which belongs as much to me as to him." At this moment, the cat spied the rat, and, jumping to the ground, soon convinced him that he was not an elephant.

Because we are like the great in one respect we must not think we are like them in all.

The Fisherman Piping

A Fisherman skilled in music took his flute and his nets to the sea-shore. Standing on a projecting rock he played several tunes, in the hope that the fish, attracted by his melody, would of their own accord dance into his net, which he had placed below. At last, having long waited in vain, he laid aside his flute, and casting his net into the sea, made an excellent haul.

The Wolf and the House-dog

A Wolf, meeting with a big, well-fed Mastiff, having a wooden collar about his neck, inquired of him who it was that fed him so well, and yet compelled him to drag that heavy log about wherever he went. "The master," he replied. Then, said the Wolf: "May no friend of mine ever be in such a plight; for the weight of this chain is enough to spoil the appetite."

Nothing can compensate us for the loss of our liberty.

The Eagle and the Kite

An Eagle, overwhelmed with sorrow, sat upon the branches of a tree, in company with a Kite. "Why," said the Kite, "do I see you with such a rueful look?" "I seek," she replied, "for a mate suitable for me, and am not able to find one." "Take me," returned the Kite; "I am much stronger than you are." "Why,

are you able to secure the means of living by your plunder?" "Well, I have often caught and carried away an ostrich in my talons." The Eagle, persuaded by these words, accepted him as her mate. Shortly after the nuptials, the Eagle said: "Fly off, and bring me back the ostrich you promised me." The Kite, soaring aloft into the air, brought back the shabbiest possible mouse. "Is this," said the Eagle, "the faithful fulfillment of your promise to me?" The Kite replied: "That I might attain to your royal hand, there is nothing that I would not have promised, however much I knew that I must fail in the performance."

Promises of a suitor must be taken with caution.

The Dogs and the Hides

Some Dogs, famished with hunger, saw some cow-hides steeping in a river. Not being able to reach them, they agreed to drink up the river; but it fell out that they burst themselves with drinking long before they reached the hides.

Attempt not impossibilities.

The Fisherman and the Little Fish

A Fisherman who lived on the produce of his nets, one day caught a single small fish as the result of his day's labor. The fish, panting convulsively, thus entreated for his life: "O Sir, what good can I be to you, and how little am I worth! I am not yet come to my full size. Pray spare my life, and put me back into the sea. I shall soon become a large fish, fit for the tables of the rich; and then you can catch me again, and make a handsome profit of me." The fisherman replied: "I should be a very simple fellow, if I were to forego my certain gain for an uncertain profit."

The Ass and his Purchaser

A man wished to purchase an Ass, and agreed with its owner that he should try him before he bought him. He took the Ass home, and put him in the straw-yard with his other Asses, upon which he left all the others, and joined himself at once to the most idle and the greatest eater of them all. The man put a halter on him, and led him back to his owner, saying: "I do not need a trial; I know that he will be just such another as the one whom he chose for his companion."

A man is known by the company he keeps.

The Shepherd and the Sheep

A Shepherd, driving his Sheep to a wood, saw an oak of unusual size, full of acorns, and, spreading his cloak under the branches, he climbed up into the tree, and shook down the acorns. The sheep, eating the acorns, frayed and tore the cloak. The Shepherd coming down, and seeing what was done, said: "O you most ungrateful creatures! you provide wool to make garments for all other men, but you destroy the clothes of him who feeds you."

The basest ingratitude is that which injures those who serve us.

The Fox and the Crow

A Crow, having stolen a bit of flesh, perched in a tree, and held it in her beak. A Fox, seeing her, longed to possess himself of the flesh, and by a wily stratagem succeeded. "How handsome is the Crow," he exclaimed, "in the beauty of her shape and in the fairness of her complexion! Oh, if her voice were only equal to her beauty, she would deservedly be considered the Queen of Birds!" This he said deceitfully, having greater admiration for the meat than for the crow. But the Crow, all her vanity aroused by the cunning flattery, and anxious to refute the reflection cast upon her voice, set up a loud caw, and dropped the flesh. The Fox quickly picked it up, and thus addressed the Crow: "My good Crow, your voice is right enough, but your wit is wanting."

He who listens to flattery is not wise, for it has no good purpose.

The Swallow and the Crow

The Swallow and the Crow had a contention about their plumage. The Crow put an end to the dispute by saying: "Your feathers are all very well in the spring, but mine protect me against the winter."

Fine weather friends are not worth much.

The Hen and the Golden Eggs

A Cottager and his wife had a Hen, which laid every day a golden egg. They supposed that it must contain a great lump of gold in its inside, and killed it in order that they might get it, when, to their surprise, they found that the Hen differed in no respect from their other hens. The foolish pair, thus hoping to become rich all at once, deprived themselves of the gain of which they were day by day assured.

The Old Man and Death

An old man was employed in cutting wood in the forest, and, in carrying the fagots into the city for sale. One day, being very wearied with his long journey, he sat down by the wayside, and, throwing down his load, besought "Death" to come. "Death" immediately appeared, in answer to his summons, and asked for what reason he had called him. The old man replied: "That, lifting up the load, you may place it again upon my shoulders."

We do not always like to be taken at our word.

The Fox and the Leopard

The Fox and the Leopard disputed which was the more beautiful of the two. The Leopard exhibited one by one the various spots which decorated his skin. The Fox, interrupting him, said: "And how much more beautiful than you am I, who am decorated, not in body, but in mind."

People are not to be judged by their coats.

The Mountain in Labor

A Mountain was once greatly agitated. Loud groans and noises were heard; and crowds of people came from all parts to see what was the matter. While they were assembled in anxious expectation of some terrible calamity, out came a Mouse.

Don't make much ado about nothing.

The Sick Kite

A Kite, sick unto death, said to his mother: "O Mother! do not mourn, but at once invoke the gods that my life may be prolonged." She replied: "Alas! my son, which of the gods do you think will pity you? Is there one whom you have not outraged by filching from their very altars a part of the sacrifice which had been offered up to them?"

We must make friends in prosperity, if we would have their help in adversity.

The Bear and the Two Travelers

Two men were traveling together, when a bear suddenly met them on their path. One of them climbed up quickly into a tree, and concealed himself in the branches. The other, seeing that he must be attacked, fell flat on the ground, and when the Bear came up and felt him with his snout, and smelt him all over, he held his breath, and feigned the appearance of death as much as he could. The Bear soon left him, for it is said he will not touch a dead body. When he was quite gone, the other traveler descended from the tree, and, accosting his friend, jocularly inquired "what it was the Bear had whispered in his ear?" His friend replied: "He gave me this advice: Never travel with a friend who deserts you at the approach of danger."

Misfortune tests the sincerity of friends.

The Wolf and the Crane

A Wolf, having a bone stuck in his throat, hired a Crane, for a large sum, to put her head into his throat and draw out the bone. When the Crane had extracted the bone, and demanded the promised payment, the Wolf, grinning and grinding his teeth, exclaimed: "Why, you have surely already a sufficient recompense, in having been permitted to draw out your head in safety from the mouth and jaws of a Wolf."

In serving the wicked, expect no reward, and be thankful if you escape injury for your pains.

The Cat and the Cock

A Cat caught a Cock, and took counsel with himself how he might find a reasonable excuse for eating him. He accused him as being a nuisance to men, by crowing in the night time, and not permitting them to sleep. The Cock defended himself by saying that he did this for the benefit of men, that they might rise betimes, for their labors. The Cat replied: "Although you abound in specious apologies, I shall not remain supperless;" and he made a meal of him.

It does no good to deny those who make false accusations knowingly.

The Monkey and the Cat

A Monkey and a Cat lived in the same family, and it was hard to tell which was the greatest thief. One day, as they were roaming about together, they spied some chestnuts roasting in the ashes. "Come," said the cunning Monkey, "we shall not go without our dinner to-day. Your claws are better than mine for the purpose; you pull them out of the hot ashes and you shall have half." Pussy pulled them out one by one, burning her claws very much in doing so. When she had stolen them all, she found that the Monkey had eaten every one.

A thief cannot be trusted, even by another thief.

The Wolf and the Horse

A Wolf coming out of a field of oats met with a Horse, and thus addressed him: "I would advise you to go into that field. It is full of capital oats, which I have left untouched for you, as you are a friend the very sound of whose teeth it will be a pleasure to me to hear." The Horse replied: "If oats had been the food for wolves, you would never have indulged your ears at the cost of your belly."

Men of evil reputation, when they perform a good deed, fail to get credit for it.

The Two Soldiers and the Robber

Two Soldiers, traveling together, were set upon by a Robber. The one fled away; the other stood his ground, and defended himself with his stout right hand. The Robber being slain, the timid companion runs up and draws his sword, and then, throwing back his traveling cloak, says: "I'll at him, and I'll take care he shall learn whom he has attacked." On this, he who had

fought with the Robber made answer: "I only wish that you had helped me just now, even if it had been only with those words, for I should have been the more encouraged, believing them to be true; but now put up your sword in its sheath and hold your equally useless tongue, till you can deceive others who do not know you. I, indeed, who have experienced with what speed you ran away, know right well that no dependence can be placed on your valor."

When a coward is once found out, his pretensions of valor are useless.

The Two Frogs

Two frogs dwelt in the same pool. The pool being dried up under the summer's heat, they left it and set out together for another home. As they went along they chanced to pass a deep well, amply supplied with water, on seeing which, one of the Frogs said to the other: "Let us descend and make our abode in this well." The other replied with greater caution: "But suppose the water should fail us, how can we get out again from so great a depth?"

Do nothing without a regard to the consequences.

The Vine and the Goat

A Vine was luxuriant in the time of vintage with leaves and grapes. A Goat, passing by, nibbled its young tendrils and its leaves. The Vine said: "Why do you thus injure me and crop my leaves? Is there no young grass left? But I shall not have to wait long for my just revenge; for if you now crop my leaves, and cut me down to my root, I shall provide the wine to pour over you when you are led as a victim to the sacrifice."

Retribution is certain.

The Mouse and the Boasting Rat

A Mouse lived in a granary which became, after a while, the frequent resort of a Cat. The Mouse was in great fear and did not know what to do. In her strait, she bethought herself of a Rat who lived not far away, and who had said in her hearing a hundred times that he was not afraid of any cat living. She resolved to visit the bold Rat and ask him to drive the Cat away. She found the Rat in his hole and relating her story, besought his help. "Pooh!" said the Rat, "You should be bold as I am; go straight about your affairs, and do not mind the Cat. I will soon follow you, and drive him away." He thought, now, he must do something to make good his boast. So he collected all the Rats in the neighborhood, resolved to frighten the Cat by numbers. But when they all came to the granary, they found that the Cat had already caught the foolish Mouse, and a single growl from him sent them all scampering to their holes.

Do not rely upon a boaster.

The Thief and the House-Dog

A Thief came in the night to break into a house. He brought with him several slices of meat, that he might pacify the House-dog, so that he should not alarm his master by barking. As the Thief threw him the pieces of meat, the Dog said: "If you think to stop my mouth, to relax my vigilance, or even to gain my regard by these gifts, you will be greatly mistaken. This sudden kindness at your hands will only make me more watchful, lest under these unexpected favors to myself you have some private ends to accomplish for your own benefit, and for my master's injury. Besides, this is not the time that I

am usually fed, which makes me all the more suspicions of your intentions."

He who offers bribes needs watching, for his intentions are not honest.

The Dogs and the Fox

Some Dogs, finding the skin of a lion, began to tear it in pieces with their teeth. A Fox, seeing them, said: "If this lion were alive, you would soon find out that his claws were stronger than your teeth."

It is easy to kick a man that is down.

The Sick Stag

A sick Stag lay down in a quiet corner of his pasture-ground. His companions came in great numbers to inquire after his health, and each one helped himself to a share of the food which had been placed for his use; so that he died, not from his sickness, but from the failure of the means of living.

Evil companions bring more hurt than profit.

The Fowler and the Ringdove

A Fowler took his gun, and went into the woods a shooting. He spied a Ringdove among the branches of an oak, and intended to kill it. He clapped the piece to his shoulder, and took his aim accordingly. But, just as he was going to pull the trigger, an adder, which he had trod upon under the grass, stung him so painfully in the leg that he was forced to quit his design, and threw his gun down in a passion. The poison immediately infected his blood, and his whole body began to mortify; which, when he perceived, he could not help owning it to be just. "Fate," said he, "has brought destruction upon me while I was contriving the death of another."

Men often fall into the trap which they prepare for others.

The Kid and the Wolf

A Kid, returning without protection from the pasture, was pursued by a Wolf. He turned round, and said to the Wolf: "I know, friend Wolf, that I must be your prey; but before I die, I would ask of you one favor, that you will play me a tune, to which I may dance." The Wolf complied, and while he was piping, and the Kid was dancing, the hounds, hearing the sound, came up and gave chase to the Wolf. The Wolf, turning to the Kid, said: "It is just what I deserve; for I, who am only a butcher, should not have turned piper to please you."

Every one should keep his own colors.

The Geese and the Cranes

The Geese and the Cranes fed in the same meadow. A bird-catcher came to ensnare them in his nets. The Cranes, being light of wing, fled away at his approach; while the Geese, being slower of flight and heavier in their bodies, were captured.

Those who are caught are not always the most guilty.

The Blind Man and the Whelp

A Blind Man was accustomed to distinguish different animals by touching them with his hands. The whelp of a Wolf was brought him, with a request that he would feel it, and say what it was. He felt it, and being in doubt, said: "I do not quite know whether it is the cub of a Fox, or the whelp of a Wolf; but this I know full well, that it would not be safe to admit him to the sheepfold."

Evil tendencies are shown early in life.

The North Wind and the Sun

The North Wind and the Sun disputed which was the more powerful, and agreed that he should be declared the victor who could first strip a wayfaring man of his clothes. The North Wind first tried his power, and blew with all his might; but the keener became his blasts, the closer the Traveler wrapped his cloak around him, till at last, resigning all hope of victory, he called upon the Sun to see what he could do. The Sun suddenly shone out with all his warmth. The Traveler no sooner felt his genial rays than he took off one garment after another, and at last, fairly overcome with heat, undressed, and bathed in a stream that lay in his path.

Persuasion is better than Force.

The Laborer and the Snake

A Snake, having made his hole close to the porch of a cottage, inflicted a severe bite on the Cottager's infant son, of which he died, to the great grief of his parents. The father resolved to kill the Snake, and the next day, on its coming out of its hole for food, took up his axe; but, making too much haste to hit him as he wriggled away, missed his head, and cut off only the end of his tail. After some time, the Cottager, afraid lest the Snake should bite him also, endeavored to make peace, and placed some bread and salt in his hole. The Snake said: "There can henceforth be no peace between us; for whenever I see you I shall remember the loss of my tail, and whenever you see me you will be thinking of the death of your son."

It is hard to forget injuries in the presence of him who caused the injury.

The Bull and the Calf

A Bull was striving with all his might to squeeze himself through a narrow passage which led to his stall. A young Calf came up and offered to go before and show him the way by which he could manage to pass. "Save yourself the trouble," said the Bull; "I knew that way long before you were born."

Do not presume to teach your elders.

The Goat and the Ass

A Man once kept a Goat and an Ass. The Goat, envying the Ass on account of his greater abundance of food, said: "How shamefully you are treated; at one time grinding in the mill, and at another carrying heavy burdens;" and he further advised him that he should pretend to be epileptic, and fall into a deep ditch and so obtain rest. The Ass gave credence to his words, and, falling into a ditch, was very much bruised. His master, sending for a leech, asked his advice. He bade him pour upon the wounds the blood of a Goat. They at once killed the Goat, and so healed the Ass.

In injuring others we are apt to receive a greater injury.

The Boasting Traveler

A Man who had traveled in foreign lands boasted very much, on returning to his own country, of the many wonderful and heroic things he had done in the different places he had visited. Among other things, he said that when he was at Rhodes he had leaped to such a distance that no man of his day could leap anywhere near him— and as to that there were in Rhodes many persons who saw him do it, and whom he could call as witnesses. One of the bystanders, interrupting him, said: "Now, my good man, if this be all true, there is no need of witnesses. Suppose this to be Rhodes and now for your leap."

Cure a boaster by putting his words to the test.

The Ass, the Cock, and the Lion

An Ass and a Cock were together, when a Lion, desperate from hunger, approached. He was about to spring upon the Ass, when the Cock (to the sound of whose voice the Lion, it is said, has a singular aversion) crowed loudly, and the Lion fled away. The Ass, observing his trepidation at the mere crowing of a cock, summoned courage to attack him, and galloped after him for that purpose. He had run no long distance when the Lion, turning about, seized him and tore him to pieces.

False confidence often leads into danger.

The Stag and the Fawn

A Stag, grown old and mischievous, was, according to custom, stamping with his foot, making offers with his head, and bellowing so terribly that the whole herd quaked for fear of him; when one of the little Fawns, coming up, addressed him thus: "Pray, what is the reason that you, who are so formidable at all other times, if you do but hear the cry of the hounds, are ready to fly out of your skin for fear?" "What you observe is true," replied the Stag, "though I know not how to account for it. I am indeed vigorous and able, and often resolve that nothing shall ever dismay my courage; but, alas! I no sooner hear the voice of a hound but my spirits fail me, and I cannot help making off as fast as my legs can carry me."

The greatest braggarts are the greatest cowards.

The Partridge and the Fowler

A Fowler caught a Partridge, and was about to kill him. The Partridge earnestly besought him to spare his life, saying: "Pray, master, permit me to live, and I will entice many Partridges to you in recompense for your mercy to me." The Fowler replied: "I shall now with the less scruple take your life, because you are willing to save it at the cost of betraying your friends and relations;" and without more ado he twisted his neck and put him in his bag with his other game.

Those who would sacrifice their friends to save themselves from harm are not entitled to mercy.

The Farmer and the Stork

A Farmer placed his nets on his newly sown plough lands, and caught a quantity of Cranes, which came to pick up his seed. With them he trapped a Stork also. The Stork, having his leg fractured by the net, earnestly besought the Farmer to spare his life. "Pray, save me, Master," he said, "and let me go free this once. My broken limb should excite your pity. Besides, I am no Crane, I am a Stork, a bird of excellent character; and see how I love and slave for my father and mother. Look too at my feathers, they are not the least like to those of a Crane." The Farmer laughed aloud, and said: "It may be all as you say; I only know this, I have taken you with these robbers, the Cranes, and you must die in their company."

Birds of a feather flock together.

The Ass and his Driver

An Ass, being driven along the high road, suddenly started off, and bolted to the brink of a deep precipice. When he was in the act of throwing himself over, his owner, seizing him by the tail, endeavored to pull him back. The Ass persisting in his effort, the man let him go, and said: "Conquer; but conquer to your cost."

The perverse generally come to harm.

The Kites and the Swans

The Kites of old time had, equally with the Swans, the privilege of song. But having heard the neigh of the horse, they were so enchanted with the sound, that they tried to imitate it; and, in trying to neigh, they forgot how to sing.

The desire for imaginary benefits often involves the loss of present blessings.

The Hare and the Hound

A Hound having started a Hare from his form, after a long run, gave up the chase. A Goat-herd, seeing him stop, mocked him, saying: "The little one is the best runner of the two." The hound replied; "You do not see the difference between us; I was only running for a dinner, but he for his life."

Incentive spurs effort.

The Dog in the Manger

A Dog lay in a manger, and by his growling and snapping prevented the oxen from eating the hay which had been placed for them. "What a selfish Dog!" said one of them to his companions; "he cannot eat the hay himself, and yet refuses to allow those to eat who can."

We should not deprive others of blessings because we cannot enjoy them ourselves.

The Crow and the Serpent

A Crow, in great want of food, saw a Serpent asleep in a sunny nook, and flying down, greedily seized him. The Serpent, turning about, bit the Crow with a mortal wound. The Crow in the agony of death exclaimed: "O unhappy me! who have found in that which I deemed a most happy windfall the source of my certain destruction."

What seem to be blessings are not always so.

The Cat and the Fox

As the Cat and the Fox were talking politics together, Reynard said: "Let things turn out ever so bad, he did not care, for he had a thousand tricks for them yet, before they should hurt him." "But pray," says he, "Mrs. Puss, suppose there should be an invasion, what course do you design to take?" "Nay," says the Cat, "I have but one shift for it, and if that won't do, I am undone." "I am sorry for you," replies Reynard, "with all my heart, and would gladly help you, but indeed, neighbor, as times go, it is not good to trust; we must even be every one for himself, as the saying is." These words were scarcely out of his mouth, when they were alarmed with a pack of hounds, that came upon them in full cry. The Cat, by the help of her single shift, ran up a tree, and sat securely among the top branches; from whence she beheld Reynard, who had not been able to get out of sight, overtaken with his thousand tricks, and torn in as many pieces by the dogs which had surrounded him.

A little common sense is often of more value than much cunning.

The Prophet

A Wizard, sitting in the market-place, told the fortunes of the passers-by. A person ran up in great haste, and announced to him that the doors of his house had been broken open, and that all his goods were being stolen. He sighed heavily, and hastened away as fast as he could run. A neighbor saw him running, and said: "Oh! you follow those? you say you can foretell the fortunes of others; how is it you did not foresee your own?"

The Eagle and the Arrow

An Eagle sat on a lofty rock, watching the movements of a Hare, whom he sought to make his prey. An archer, who saw him from a place of concealment, took an accurate aim, and wounded him mortally. The Eagle gave one look at the arrow that had entered his heart, and saw in that single glance that its feathers had been furnished by himself. "It is a double grief to me," he exclaimed, "that I should perish by an arrow feathered from my own wings."

The misfortunes arising from a man's own misconduct are the hardest to bear.

The Dog Invited to Supper

A Gentleman, having prepared a great feast, invited a Friend to supper; and the Gentleman's Dog, meeting the Friend's Dog, "Come," said he, "my good fellow, and sup with us to-night." The Dog was delighted with the invitation, and as he stood by and saw the preparations for the feast, said to himself: "Capital fare indeed! this is, in truth, good luck. I shall revel in dainties, and I will take good care to lay in an ample stock to-night, for I may have nothing to eat to-morrow." As he said this to himself, he wagged his tail, and gave a sly look at his friend who had incited him. But his tail wagging to and fro caught the cook's eye, who, seeing a stranger, straightway seized him by the legs, and threw him out the window to the street below. When he reached the ground, he set off yelping

down the street; upon which the neighbors' dogs ran up to him and asked him how he liked his supper. "In faith," said he, with a sorry smile, "I hardly know, for we drank so deeply, that I can't even tell you which way I got out."

Those who enter by the back stairs must not complain if they are thrown out by the window.

The Frogs Asking for a King

The Frogs, grieved at having no established Ruler, sent ambassadors to Jupiter entreating for a King. He, perceiving their simplicity, cast down a huge log into the lake. The Frogs, terrified at the splash occasioned by its fall, hid themselves in the depth of the pool. But no sooner did they see that the huge log continued motionless, than they swam again to the top of the water, dismissed their fears, and came so to despise it as to climb up, and to squat upon it. After some time they began to think themselves ill-treated in the appointment of so inert a Ruler, and sent a second deputation to Jupiter to pray that he would set over them another sovereign. He then gave them an Eel to govern them. When the Frogs discovered his easy good-nature, they yet a third time sent to Jupiter to beg that he would once more choose for them another King. Jupiter, displeased at their complaints, sent a Heron, who preyed upon the Frogs day by day, till there were none left to complain. When you seek to change your condition, be sure that you can better it.

The Dog and the Hare

A Hound, having started a Hare on the hill-side, pursued her for some distance, at one time biting her with his teeth as if he would take her life, and at another time fawning upon her, as if in play with another dog. The Hare said to him: "I wish you would act sincerely by me, and show yourself in your true colors. If you are a friend, why do you bite me so hard? If an enemy, why do you fawn on me?"

They are no friends whom you know not whether to trust or to distrust.

The Dog and his Master's Dinner

A Dog had been taught to take his master's dinner to him every day. As he smelled the good things in the basket, he was sorely tempted to taste them, but he resisted the temptation and continued day after day to carry the basket faithfully. One day all the dogs in the neighborhood followed him with longing eyes and greedy jaws, and tried to steal the dinner from the basket. At first the faithful dog tried to run away from them, but they pressed him so close that at last he stopped to argue with them. This was what the thieves desired, and they soon ridiculed him to that extent that he said: "Very well, I will divide with you," and he seized the best piece of chicken in the basket, and left the rest for the others to enjoy.

He who stops to parley with temptation, will be very likely to yield.

The Buffoon and the Countryman

A rich nobleman once opened the theater to the public without charge, and gave notice that he would handsomely reward any one who would produce a new amusement. A Buffoon, well known for his jokes, said that he had a kind of entertainment that had never been produced in a theater. This report, being spread about, created a great stir in the place, and the theater was crowded to see the new entertainment. The Buffoon appeared, and imitated the squeaking of a little pig so admirably with his voice, that the audience declared that he had a porker under his cloak,

and demanded that it should be shaken out. When that was done, and yet nothing was found, they cheered the actor, with the loudest applause. A countryman in the crowd proclaimed that he would do the same thing on the next day. On the morrow a still larger crowd assembled in the theater. Both of the performers appeared on the stage. The Buffoon grunted and squeaked, and obtained, as on the preceding day, the applause and cheers of the spectators. Next the Countryman commenced, and pretending that he concealed a little pig beneath his clothes (which in truth he did), contrived to lay hold of and to pull his ear, when he began to squeak. The crowd, however, cried out that the Buffoon had given a far more exact imitation. On this the Rustic produced the pig, and showed them the greatness of their mistake.

Critics are not always to be depended upon.

The Boar and the Ass

A little scoundrel of an Ass, happening to meet with a Boar, had a mind to be arch upon him, and so, says he: "Your humble servant." The Boar, somewhat nettled at his familiarity, bristled up to him, and told him he was surprised to hear him utter so impudent an untruth, and was just going to show his resentment by giving him a rip in the flank; but wisely stifling his passion, he contented himself with saying: "Go, you sorry beast! I do not care to foul my tusks with the blood of so base a creature."

Dignity cannot afford to quarrel with its inferiors.

The Fox and the Goat

A Fox, having fallen into a well, could find no means of escape. A Goat, overcome with thirst, came to the well, and, seeing the Fox, inquired if the water was good. The Fox, concealing his sad plight under a merry guise, indulged in lavish praise of the water, saying it was beyond measure excellent, and encouraged him to descend. The Goat, mindful only of

his thirst, thoughtlessly jumped down, when, just as he quenched his thirst, the Fox informed him of the difficulty they were both in, and suggested a scheme for their common escape. "If," said he, "you will place your fore-feet upon the wall, and bend your head, I will run up your back and escape, and will help you out." On the Goat readily assenting to this proposal, the Fox leaped upon his back, and steadying himself with the goat's horns reached in safety the mouth of the well, and immediately made off as fast as he could. The Goat upbraided him with the breach of his bargain, when he turned round and cried out: "You foolish fellow! If you had as many brains in your head as you have hairs in your beard, you would never have gone down before you had inspected the way up, nor have exposed yourself to dangers from which you had determined upon no means of escape."

Look before you leap.

The Oxen and the Butchers

The Oxen, once on a time, sought to destroy the Butchers, who practiced a trade destructive to their race. They assembled on a certain day to carry out their purpose, and sharpened their horns for the contest. One of them, an exceedingly old one (for many a field had he ploughed), thus spoke: "These Butchers, it is true, slaughter us, but they do so with skillful hands, and with no unnecessary pain. If we get rid of them, we shall fall into the hands of unskillful operators, and thus suffer a double death; for you may be assured

that, though all the Butchers should perish, yet will men never want beef."

Do not be in a hurry to change one evil for another.

The Horse and his Rider

A Horse-soldier took great pains with his charger. As long as the war lasted, he looked upon him as his fellow-helper in all emergencies, and fed him carefully with hay and corn. When the war was over, he only allowed him chaff to eat, and made him carry heavy loads of wood, and subjected him to much slavish drudgery and ill-treatment. War, however, being again proclaimed, the Soldier put on his charger its military trappings, and mounted, being clad in his heavy coat of mail. The Horse fell down straightway under the weight, no longer equal to the burden, and said to his master: "You must now e'en go to the war on foot, for you have transformed me from a Horse into an Ass."

He who slights his friends when they are not needed must not expect them to serve him when he needs them.

The Fawn and his Mother

A young Fawn once said to his mother: "You are larger than a dog, and swifter, and more used to running; why, then, O Mother! are you always in such a terrible fright of the hounds?" She smiled, and said: "I know full well, my son, that all you say is true. I have the advantages you mention, but yet when I hear the bark of a single dog I feel ready to faint."

No arguments will give courage to the coward.

The Lark and her Young Ones

A Lark had made her nest in the young green wheat. The brood had almost grown, when the owner of the field, overlooking his crop, said: "I must send to all my neighbors to help me with my harvest." One of the young Larks heard him, and asked his mother to what place they should move for safety. "There is no occasion to move yet, my son," she replied. The owner of the field came a few days later, and said: "I will come myself to-morrow, and will get in the harvest." Then the Lark said to her brood: "It is time now to be off—he no longer trusts to his friends, but will reap the field himself."

Self-help is the best help.

The Bowman and the Lion

A very skillful Bowman went to the mountains in search of game. All the beasts of the forest fled at his approach. The Lion alone challenged him to combat. The Bowman immediately let fly an arrow; and said to the Lion: "I send thee my messenger, that from him thou mayest learn what I myself shall be when I assail thee." The Lion, thus wounded, rushed, away in great fear, and on a Fox exhorting him to be of good courage, and not to run away at the first attack, he replied: "You counsel me in vain, for if he sends so

fearful a messenger, how shall I abide the attack of the man himself?"

A man who can strike from a distance is no pleasant neighbor.

The Boy and the Filberts

A Boy put his hand into a pitcher full of filberts. He grasped as many as he could possibly hold, but when he endeavored to pull out his hand, he was prevented from doing so by the neck of the pitcher, which was much smaller than his closed hand. Unwilling to lose his filberts, and yet unable to withdraw his hand, he burst into tears, and bitterly lamented his disappointment. A bystander said to him: "Be satisfied with half the quantity, and you will readily draw out your hand."

Do not attempt too much at once.

The Woman and her Hen

A Woman possessed a Hen that gave her an egg every day. She often thought with herself how she might obtain two eggs daily instead of one, and at last, to gain her purpose, determined to give the Hen a double allowance of barley. From that day the Hen became fat and sleek, and never once laid another egg.

Covetousness overreacheth itself.

The Heifer and the Ox

A Heifer saw an Ox hard at work harnessed to a plough, and tormented him with reflections on his unhappy fate in being compelled to labor. Shortly afterward, at the harvest home, the owner released the Ox from his yoke, but bound the Heifer with cords, and led her away to the altar to be slain in honor of the festival. The Ox saw what was being done, and said to the Heifer: "For this you were allowed to live in idleness, because you were presently to be sacrificed."

The lives of the idle can best be spared.

The Lamb and the Wolf

A Wolf pursued a Lamb, which fled for refuge to a certain temple. The Wolf called out to him and said: "The priest will slay you in sacrifice, if he should catch you;" on which the Lamb replied: "It would be better for me to be sacrificed in the temple, than to be eaten by you."

It is safer to be among friends than enemies.

The Bear and the Gardener

A Gardener, who lived alone, became discontented, and set out, one day, to seek a friend who would be a suitable companion. He had not gone far when he met a Bear, whom he invited to come and live with him. The Bear was a very silly one, who was also

discontented with living alone, so he went home with the Gardener very willingly. The Gardener provided all the food, and the only service he required of the Bear was to keep the flies off his face while he slept in the shade. One day, a fly insisted upon lighting on the Gardener's face, although he was brushed off again and again. The silly Bear finally became so enraged that he threw a heavy stone upon it. He killed the fly, but, alas! he also killed his friend.

Better have no friend at all than a foolish one.

The Eagle and the Fox

An Eagle and a Fox formed an intimate friendship, and decided to live near each other. The Eagle built her nest in a tall tree, while the Fox crept into the underwood and there produced her young. Not long after, when the Fox was ranging for food, the Eagle, being in want of provision for her young ones, swooped down and seized upon one of the little cubs, and feasted herself and brood. The Fox on her return, discovering what had happened, was less grieved for the death of her young than for her inability to avenge them. A just retribution, however, quickly fell upon the Eagle. While hovering near an altar, on which some villagers were sacrificing a goat, she suddenly seized a piece of flesh, and carried with it to her nest a burning cinder. A strong breeze soon fanned the spark into a flame, and the eaglets, as yet unfledged and helpless, were roasted in their nest and dropped down dead at the bottom of the tree. The Fox gobbled them up in the sight of the Eagle.

The tyrant is never safe from those whom he oppresses.

The Hawk and the Nightingale

A Nightingale, sitting aloft upon an oak, was seen by a Hawk, who made a swoop down, and seized him. The Nightingale earnestly besought the Hawk to let him go, saying that he was not big enough to satisfy the hunger of a Hawk, who ought to pursue the larger birds. The Hawk said: "I should indeed have lost my senses if I should let go food ready to my hand, for the sake of pursuing birds which are not yet even within sight."

A bird in the hand is worth two in the bush.

The Hen and the Swallow

A Hen finding the eggs of a viper, and carefully keeping them warm, nourished them into life. A Swallow observing what she had done, said: "You silly creature! Why have you hatched these vipers, which, when they shall have grown, will surely inflict injury on all of us, beginning with yourself?"

If we nourish evil, it will sooner or later turn upon us.

The Herdsman and the Lost Bull

A Herdsman, tending kine in a forest, lost a Bull-calf from the fold. After a long and fruitless search, he made a vow that, if he could only discover the thief who had stolen the Calf he would offer a lamb in sacrifice to the Guardian Deities of the forest. Not long afterwards, as he ascended a small hillock, he saw at its foot a Lion feeding on the Calf. Terrified at the sight, he lifted his eyes and his hands to heaven, and said: "Just now I vowed to offer a lamb to the Guardian Deities of the forest if I could only find out who had robbed me; but now that I have discovered the thief, I would willingly add a full-grown Bull to the Calf I have lost, and give them both to the guardians of the forest, if I may only secure my own escape from this terrible Lion in safety."

That which we are anxious to find, we are sometimes even more anxious to escape from, when we have succeeded in finding it.

The Hawk, the Kite, and the Pigeons

The Pigeons, terrified by the appearance of a Kite, called upon the Hawk to defend them. He at once consented. When they had admitted him into the cote, they found that he made more havoc and slew a larger number of them in a single day, than the Kite could possibly pounce upon in a whole year.

Avoid a remedy that is worse than the disease.

The Farmer and the Cranes

Some Cranes made their feeding grounds on some plough-lands newly sown with wheat. For a long time the Farmer, brandishing an empty sling, chased them away by the terror he inspired; but when the birds found that the sling was only swung in the air, they ceased to take any notice of it, and would not move. The farmer, on seeing this, charged his sling with stones, and killed a great number. They at once forsook his plough-lands, and cried to each other: "It is time for us to be off, for this man is no longer content to scare us, but begins to show us in earnest what he can do."

If words suffice not, blows must follow.

The Cat and the Mice

A certain house was overrun with Mice. A Cat, discovering this, made her way into it, and began to catch and eat them one by one. The Mice, being continually devoured, kept themselves close in their holes. The Cat, no longer able to get at them, perceived that she must tempt them forth by some device. For this purpose she jumped upon a peg, and, suspending herself from it, pretended to be dead. When the Mice came near she pounced among them and killed a great number. Pleased with the success of the trick, she tried another. She whitened herself with flour, and lay still on the heap of bags, as though she was one of them. The young Mice crept dangerously near her, but an old one peeping stealthily out said: "Ah, my good madam, though you should turn into a real flour-bag, I will not come too near you."

Avoid even appearances of danger.

The Father and his Sons

A Father had a family of sons who were perpetually quarreling among themselves. When he failed to heal their disputes by his exhortations, he one day told them to bring him a bundle of sticks. When they had done so, he placed the bundle into the hands of each of them in succession, and ordered them to break it in pieces. They each tried with all their strength, and were not able to do it. He next unclosed the faggot, and took the sticks, separately, one by one, and again put them into their hands, on which they broke them easily. He then addressed them in these words: "My sons, if you are of one mind, and unite to assist each other, you will be as this faggot, uninjured by all attempts of your enemies; but if you are divided among yourselves, you will be broken as easily as these sticks."

Disunited families are easily injured by others.

The Fox and the Grapes

A famished Fox saw some clusters of ripe black grapes hanging from a trellised vine. She resorted to all her tricks to get at them, but wearied herself in vain, for she could not reach them. At last she turned away, beguiling herself of her disappointment, and saying: "The Grapes are sour, and not ripe as I thought."

Revile not things beyond your reach.

The Owl and the Grasshopper

An Owl who was sitting in a hollow tree, dozing away a summer's afternoon, was very much disturbed by a rogue of a Grasshopper singing in the grass beneath. So far from keeping quiet, or moving away at the request of the Owl, the Grasshopper sang all the more, and called her an old blinker, that only came out at night when all honest people had gone to bed. The Owl waited in silence for a time, and then artfully addressed the Grasshopper as follows: "Well, my dear, if one cannot be allowed to sleep, it is something to be kept awake by such a pleasant voice. And now I think of it, I have a bottle of delicious nectar. If you will come up, you shall have a drop." The silly Grasshopper, came hopping up to the Owl, who at once caught and killed him, and finished her nap in comfort.

Flattery is not a proof of admiration.

The Ass carrying the Image

An Ass once carried through the streets of the city a famous wooden Image, to be placed in one of its temples. The crowd as he passed along made lowly prostration before the Image. The Ass, thinking that they bowed their heads in token of respect for him, bristled up with pride and gave himself airs, and refused to move another step. The driver, seeing him thus stop, laid his whip lustily about his shoulders and said: "O you perverse dull-head! it is not yet come to this, that men pay worship to an Ass."

They are not wise who take to themselves the credit due to others.

The Ass and the Lap-Dog

A man had an Ass and a Maltese Lap-dog, a very great beauty. The Ass was left in a stable, and had plenty of oats and hay to eat, just as any other Ass would. The Lap-dog was a great favorite with his master, and he frisked and jumped about him in a manner pleasant to see. The Ass had much work to do, in grinding the corn-mill, and in carrying wood from the forest or burdens from the farm. He often lamented his own hard fate, and contrasted it with the luxury and idleness of the Lap-dog, till

at last one day he broke his halter, and galloped into his master's house, kicking up his heels without measure, and frisking and fawning as well as he could. He next tried to jump about his master as he had seen the Lap-dog do, but he broke the table and smashed all the dishes upon it to atoms. He then attempted to lick his master, and jumped upon his back. The servants hearing the strange hubbub, and perceiving the danger of their master, quickly relieved him, and drove out the Ass to his stable, with kicks, and clubs, and cuffs. The Ass, beaten nearly to death, thus lamented: "I have brought it all on myself! Why could I not have been contented to labor with my companions, and not try to live by idleness?"

The Tortoise and the Eagle

A Tortoise, lazily basking in the sun, complained to the sea-birds of her hard fate, that no one would teach her to fly. An Eagle, hovering near, heard her lamentation, and demanded what reward she would give him, if he would take her aloft, and float her in the air. "I will give you," she said, "all the riches of the Red Sea." "I will teach you to fly then," said the Eagle; and taking her up in his talons, he carried her almost to the clouds,—when suddenly letting her go, she fell on a lofty mountain, and dashed her shell to pieces. The Tortoise exclaimed in the moment of death: "I have deserved my present fate; for what had I to do with wings and clouds, who can with difficulty move about on the earth?"

If men had all they wished, they would be often ruined.

The Fox who had Lost his Tail

A Fox, caught in a trap, escaped with the loss of his "brush." Henceforth, feeling his life a burden from the shame and ridicule to which he was exposed, he schemed to bring all the other Foxes into a like condition with himself. He publicly advised them to cut off their tails, saying "that they would not only look much better without them, but that they would get rid of the weight of the brush." One of them said: "If you had not yourself lost your tail, my friend, you would not thus counsel us."

Advice prompted by selfishness should not be heeded.

The Old Lion

A Lion, worn out with years, lay on the ground at the point of death. A Boar rushed upon him, and avenged with a stroke of his tusks a long remembered injury. Shortly afterwards the Bull with his horns gored him as if he were an enemy. When the Ass saw that the huge beast could be assailed with impunity, he let drive at his forehead with his heels.

The Porcupine and the Snakes

A Porcupine, wanting to shelter himself, desired a nest of Snakes to give him admittance into their cave. They were prevailed upon, and let him in accordingly; but were so annoyed with his sharp prickly quills that they soon repented of their easy compliance, and entreated the

Porcupine to withdraw, and leave them their hole to themselves. "No," says he, "let them quit the place that don't like it; for my part, I am well enough satisfied as I am."

Hospitality is a virtue, but should be wisely exercised; we may by thoughtlessness entertain foes instead of friends.

The Ass and the Wolf

An Ass, feeding in a meadow, saw a Wolf approaching to seize him, and immediately pretended to be lame. The Wolf, coming up, inquired the cause of his lameness. The Ass said that he had a thorn in his foot, and requested the Wolf to pull it out. The Wolf consenting, the Ass with his heels kicked his teeth into his mouth, and galloped away. The Wolf said: "I am rightly served, for why did I attempt the art of healing, when my father only taught me the trade of a butcher?"

Every one to his trade.

The Horse and the Groom

A Groom used to spend whole days in currycombing and rubbing down his Horse, but at the same time stole his oats, and sold them for his own profit. "Alas!" said the Horse, "if you really wish me to be in good condition, you should groom me less, and feed me more."

If you wish to do a service, do it right.

The Ass and his Shadow

A traveler hired an Ass to convey him to a distant place. The day being intensely hot, and the sun shining in its strength, the traveler stopped to rest, and sought shelter from the heat under the Shadow of the Ass. As this afforded only protection for one, and as the traveler and the owner of the Ass both claimed it, a violent dispute arose between them as to which of them had the right to it. The owner maintained that he had let the Ass only, and not his Shadow. The traveler asserted that he had, with the hire of the Ass, hired his Shadow also. The quarrel proceeded from words to blows, and while the men fought the Ass galloped off.

In quarreling about the shadow we often lose the substance.

The Horse and the Loaded Ass

An idle Horse, and an Ass laboring under a heavy burden, were traveling the road together. The Ass, ready to faint under his heavy load, entreated the Horse to assist him, and lighten his burden, by taking some of it upon his back. The Horse was ill-natured and refused to do it; upon which the poor Ass tumbled down in the midst of the highway, and expired. The countryman then took the whole burden, and laid it upon the Horse, together with the skin of the dead Ass.

Laziness often prepares a burden for its own back.

The Mules and the Robbers

Two Mules laden with packs were trudging along. One carried panniers filled with money, the other sacks of grain. The Mule carrying the treasure walked with head erect, and tossed up and down the bells fastened to his neck. His companion followed with quiet and easy step. All on a sudden Robbers rushed from their hiding-places upon them, and in the scuffle with their owners wounded the Mule carrying the treasure, which they greedily seized upon, while they took no notice of the grain. The Mule which had been wounded bewailed his misfortunes. The other replied: "I am glad that I was thought so little of, for I have lost nothing, nor am I hurt with any wound."

The conspicuous run the greatest risk.

The Thirsty Pigeon

A Pigeon, oppressed by excessive thirst, saw a goblet of water painted on a sign-board. Not supposing it to be only a picture, she flew toward it with a loud whirr, and unwittingly dashed against the sign-board and jarred herself terribly. Having broken her wings by the blow, she fell to the ground, and was caught by one of the bystanders.

Zeal should not outrun discretion.

The Lion and the Three Bulls

Three Bulls for a long time pastured together. A Lion lay in ambush in the hope of making them his prey, but was afraid to attack them whilst they kept together. Having at last by guileful speeches succeeded in separating them, he attacked them without fear, as they fed alone, and feasted on them one by one at his own leisure.

In union is strength.

The Dog and the Shadow

A Dog, crossing a bridge over a stream with a piece of flesh in his mouth, saw his own shadow in the water, and took it for another Dog, with a piece of meat double his own in size. He therefore let go his own, and fiercely attacked the other Dog, to get his larger piece from him. He thus lost both—that which he grasped at in the water, because it was a shadow and his own, because the stream swept it away.

It is not wise to be too greedy.

The Great and the Little Fishes

A Fisherman was drawing up a net which he had cast into the sea, full of all sorts of fish. The Little Fish escaped through the meshes of the net, and got back into the deep, but the Great Fish were all caught and hauled into the ship.

Our insignificance is often the cause of our safety.

The Ants and the Grasshopper

The Ants were employing a fine winter's day in drying grain collected in the summer time. A Grasshopper, perishing with famine, passed by and earnestly begged for a little food. The Ants inquired of him: "Why did you not treasure up food during the summer?" He replied:

"I had not leisure; I passed the days in singing." They then said: "If you were foolish enough to sing all the summer, you must dance supperless to bed in the winter."

Idleness brings want.

The Wolves and the Sheep

"Why should there always be this implacable warfare between us?" said the Wolves to the Sheep. "Those evil-disposed Dogs have much to answer for. They always bark whenever we approach you, and attack us before we have done any harm. If you would only dismiss them from your heels, there might soon be treaties of peace between us." The sheep, poor silly creatures! were easily beguiled, and dismissed the Dogs. The Wolves destroyed the unguarded flock at their pleasure.

Change not friends for foes.

The Flies and the Honey

A Jar of Honey having been upset in a housekeeper's room, a number of flies were attracted by its sweetness, and placing their feet in it, ate it greedily. Their feet, however, became so smeared with the honey that they could not use their wings, nor release themselves, and were suffocated. Just as they were expiring, they exclaimed, "O foolish creatures that we are! For the sake of a little pleasure we have destroyed ourselves."

The Fox and the Stork

The Fox invited the Stork to dinner, and provided nothing but a soup, in a wide, shallow dish. This he could lap up with ease; but the Stork, who could but just dip in the point of his bill, was not a bit better. A few days after, he returned the compliment, and invited the Fox; but suffered nothing to be brought to the table but some minced meat in a glass jar, the neck of which was so deep and so narrow, that, though the Stork with his long bill could eat very well, all that the Fox could do was to lick the brims. Reynard was heartily vexed, but owned that he had been used as he deserved.

Those who practice cunning must expect to suffer by it.

The Bat and the Weasels

A Bat, falling upon the ground, was caught by a Weasel, of whom he earnestly besought his life. The Weasel refused, saying that he was by nature the enemy of all birds. The Bat assured him that he was not a bird, but a mouse, and thus saved his life. Shortly afterward the Bat again fell on the ground, and was caught by another Weasel, whom he likewise entreated not to eat him. The Weasel said that he had a special hostility to mice. The Bat assured him that he was not a mouse, but a bat; and thus a second time escaped.

The Hare and the Tortoise

A Hare one day ridiculed the short feet and slow pace of the Tortoise. The latter, laughing, said: "Though you be swift as the wind, I will beat you in a race." The Hare, deeming her assertion to be simply impossible, assented to the proposal; and they agreed that the Fox should choose the course, and fix the goal. On the day appointed for the race they started together. The Tortoise never for a moment stopped, but went on with a slow but steady pace straight to the end of the course. The Hare, trusting to his native swiftness, cared little about the race, and lying down by the wayside, fell fast asleep. At last waking up, and moving as fast as he could, he saw the Tortoise had reached the goal, and was comfortably dozing after her fatigue.

Perseverance is surer than swiftness.

Jupiter and the Monkey

Jupiter issued a proclamation to all the beasts of the forest, and promised a royal reward to the one whose offspring should be deemed the handsomest. The Monkey came with the rest, and presented, with all a mother's tenderness, a flat-nosed, hairless, ill-featured young Monkey as a candidate for the promised reward. A general laugh saluted her on the presentation of her son. She resolutely said: "I know not whether Jupiter will allot the prize to my son; but this I do know, that he is the dearest, handsomest, and most beautiful of all who are here."

A mother's love blinds her to many imperfections.

The Lion in Love

A Lion demanded the daughter of a woodcutter in marriage. The Father, unwilling to grant and yet afraid to refuse his request, hit upon this expedient. He expressed his willingness to accept him as the suitor of his daughter on one condition; that he should allow him to extract his teeth, and cut off his claws. The Lion cheerfully assented to the proposal: when, however, he next repeated his request, the woodman set upon him with his club.

The Miser

A Miser had a lump of gold which he buried in the ground, coming to look at the spot every day. One day he found that it was stolen, and he began to tear his hair and loudly lament. A neighbor, seeing him, said: "Pray do not grieve so; bury a stone in the hole, and fancy it is the gold. It will serve you just as well, for when the gold was there you made no use of it."

The Wolf and the Goat

A Wolf saw a Goat feeding at the summit of a steep precipice, where he had not a chance of reaching her. He called to her, and earnestly besought her to come lower down, lest she should by some mishap get a fall; and he added that the meadows lay where he was standing, and that the herbage was most tender. She replied: "No, my friend, it is not of me you are thinking, but of yourself."

Invitations prompted by selfishness are not to be accepted.

The Kid and the Wolf

A Kid, mounted on a high rock, bestowed all manner of abuse upon a Wolf on the ground below. The Wolf, looking up, replied: "Do not think, vain creature, that you annoy me. I regard this ill language as coming not from you, but from the place on which you stand."

The Bald Knight

A Bald Knight, who wore a wig, went out to hunt. A sudden puff of wind blew off his hat and wig, at which a loud laugh rang forth from his companions. He joined in the joke by saying: "What marvel that hairs which are not mine should fly from me, when my own have forsaken even the man with whom they were born."

Those who cannot take care of their own, should not be entrusted with the care of another's property.

The Fox and the Wood-Cutter

A Fox, running before the hounds, came across a Wood-cutter felling an oak, and besought him to show him a safe hiding-place. The Wood-cutter advised him to take shelter in his own hut. The Fox crept in, and hid himself in a corner. The Huntsman came up, with his hounds, in a few minutes, and inquired of the Wood-cutter if he had seen the Fox. He declared that he had not seen him, and yet pointed, all the time he was speaking, to the hut where the Fox lay hid. The Huntsman took no notice of the signs, but, believing

his word, hastened forward in the chase. As soon as they were well away, the Fox departed without taking any notice of the Wood-cutter; whereon he called to him, and reproached him, saying: "You ungrateful fellow, you owe your life to me, and yet you leave me without a word of thanks." The Fox replied: "Indeed, I should have thanked you most fervently, if your deeds had been as good as your words."

The Lion, the Bear, and the Fox

A Lion and a Bear seized upon a kid at the same moment, and fought fiercely for its possession. When they had fearfully lacerated each other, and were faint from the long combat, they lay down exhausted with fatigue. A Fox who had gone round them at a distance several times, saw them both stretched on the ground, and the Kid lying untouched in the middle, ran in between them, and seizing the Kid, scampered off as fast as he could. The Lion and the Bear saw him, but not being able to get up, said: "Woe betide us, that we should have fought and belabored ourselves only to serve the turn of a Fox!"

It sometimes happens that one man has all the toil, and another all the profit.

The Stag in the Ox-Stall

A Stag, hardly pressed by the hounds, and blind through fear to the danger he was running into, took shelter in a farm-yard, and hid himself in a shed among the oxen. An Ox gave him this kindly warning: "O unhappy creature! why should you thus, of your own accord, incur destruction, and trust yourself in the house of your enemy?" The Stag replied: "Do you only suffer me, friend, to stay where I am, and I will undertake to find some favorable opportunity of effecting my escape." At the

approach of the evening the herdsman came to feed his cattle, but did not see the Stag. The Stag, congratulating himself on his safety, began to express his sincere thanks to the Oxen who had kindly afforded him help in the hour of need. One of them again answered him: "We indeed wish you well, but the danger is not over. There is one other yet to pass through the shed, who has as it were a hundred eyes, and, until he has come and gone, your life is still in peril." At that moment the master himself entered, and having had to complain that his oxen had not been properly fed, he went up to their racks, and cried out: "Why is there such a scarcity of fodder? There is not half enough straw for them to lie on. Those lazy fellows have not even swept the cobwebs away." While he thus examined everything, he spied the antlers of the Stag peeping out of the straw. Summoning his laborers, he ordered that the Stag should be killed.

What is safety for one is not always safety for another.

The Eagle and the Jackdaw

An Eagle, flying down from his eyrie on a lofty rock, seized upon a lamb, and carried him aloft in his talons. A Jackdaw who witnessed the capture of the lamb, was stirred with envy, and determined to emulate the strength and flight of the Eagle. He flew round with a great whirr of his wings, and settled upon a large sheep, with the intention of carrying it off, but his claws becoming entangled in its fleece, he was unable to release himself, although he fluttered with his feathers as much as he could. The shepherd, seeing what had happened, ran up and caught him. He at once clipped his wings, and, taking him home at night, gave him to his children.

We should not permit our ambition to lead us beyond the limits of our power.

The Three Tradesmen

A great city was besieged, and its inhabitants were called together to consider the best means of protecting it from the enemy. A Bricklayer present earnestly recommended bricks, as affording the best materials for an effectual resistance. A Carpenter, with equal energy, proposed timber, as providing a preferable method of defense. Upon which a Currier stood up, and said: "Sirs, I differ from you altogether; there is no material for resistance equal to a covering of hides; and nothing so good as leather."

Every man for his trade.

The Dancing Monkeys

A Prince had some Monkeys trained to dance. Being naturally great mimics of men's actions, they showed themselves most apt pupils; and when arrayed in their rich clothes and masks, they danced as well as any of the courtiers. The spectacle was often repeated with great applause, till on one occasion a courtier, bent on mischief, took from his pocket a handful of nuts, and threw them upon the stage. The Monkeys, at the sight of the nuts, forgot their dancing, and became (as indeed they were) Monkeys instead of actors, and pulling off their masks and tearing their robes, they fought with one another for the nuts. The dancing spectacle thus came to an end, amidst the laughter and ridicule of the audience.

They who assume a character will betray themselves by their actions.

The Ass and the Grasshopper

An Ass, having heard some Grasshoppers chirping, was highly enchanted; and desiring to possess the same charms of melody, demanded what sort of food they lived on, to give them such beautiful voices. They replied: "The dew." The Ass resolved that he would live only upon dew, and in a short time died of hunger.

Where one may live, another may starve.

The Ass in the Lion's Skin

An Ass, having put on the Lion's skin, roamed about in the forest, and amused himself by frightening all the foolish animals he met with in his wanderings. At last, meeting a Fox, he tried to frighten him also, but the Fox no sooner heard the sound of his voice, than he exclaimed: "I might possibly have been frightened myself, if I had not heard your bray."

No disguise will hide one's true character.

The Boy Bathing

A Boy bathing in a river was in danger of being drowned. He called out to a traveler passing by for help. The traveler, instead of holding out a helping hand, stood up unconcernedly, and scolded the boy for his imprudence. "Oh, sir!" cried the youth, "pray help me now, and scold me afterwards."

Counsel, without help, is useless.

The Cock and the Fox

The Fox, passing early one summer's morning near a farm-yard, was caught in a springe, which the farmer had planted there for that end. The Cock, at a distance, saw what happened, and, hardly yet daring to trust himself too near so dangerous a foe, approached him cautiously, and peeped at him. Reynard addressed himself to him, with all the designing artifice imaginable. "Dear cousin," says he, "you see what an unfortunate accident has befallen me here, and all upon your account: for, as I was creeping through yonder hedge, in my way homeward, I heard you crow, and was resolved to ask you how you did before I went any farther; but I met with this disaster; and therefore now I must ask you for a knife to cut this string; or, at least, to conceal my misfortune till I have gnawed it asunder." The Cock, seeing how the case stood, made no reply, but posted away as fast as he could, and told the farmer, who came and killed the Fox.

To aid the vicious is to become a partner in their guilt.

The Viper and the File

A Viper, entering the workshop of a smith, sought from the tools the means of satisfying his hunger. He more particularly addressed himself to a File, and asked of him the favor of a meal. The File replied: "You must indeed be a simple-minded fellow if you expect to get anything from me, who am accustomed to take from every one, and never to give anything in return."

The covetous are poor givers.

The Oxen and the Axle-Trees

A heavy wagon was being dragged along a country lane by a team of oxen. The axle-trees groaned and creaked terribly, when the oxen, turning round, thus addressed the wheels: "Hallo there! why do you make so much noise? We bear all the labor, and we, not you, ought to cry out."

Those who suffer most cry out the least.

The Bear and the Bee-Hives

A Bear that had found his way into a garden where Bees were kept began to turn over the hives and devour the honey. The Bees settled in swarms about his head, and stung his eyes and nose so much, that, maddened with pain, he tore the skin from his head with his own claws.

The Thrush and the Swallow

A young Thrush, who lived in an orchard once became acquainted with a Swallow. A friendship sprang up between them; and the Swallow, after skimming the orchard and the neighboring meadow, would every now and then come and visit the Thrush. The Thrush, hopping from branch to branch, would welcome him with his most cheerful note. "O mother!" said he to his parent one day, "never had creature such a friend as I have in this same Swallow."—"Nor ever any mother," replied the parent-bird, "such a silly son as I have in this same Thrush. Long before the approach of winter, your friend will have left you; and while you sit shivering on a leafless bough he will be sporting under sunny skies hundreds of miles away."

The Sensible Ass

An Old Fellow, in time of war, was allowing his Ass to feed in a green meadow, when he was alarmed by a sudden advance of the enemy. He tried every means in his power to urge the Ass to fly, but in vain. "The enemy are upon us!" said he. "And what will the enemy do?" asked the Ass. "Will they put two pairs of panniers on my back, instead of one?"—"No," answered the Man; "there is no fear of that."—"Why, then," replied the Ass, "I'll not stir an inch. I am born to be a slave; and my greatest enemy is he who gives me most to carry."

The Lion and the Ass

A Lion and an Ass made an agreement to go out hunting together. By-and-by they came to a cave, where wild goats abode. The Lion took up his station at the mouth of the cave, and the Ass, going within, kicked and brayed, and made a mighty fuss to frighten them out. When the Lion had caught them, the Ass came out and asked him if he had not made a noble fight. "Yes, indeed," said the Lion; "and I assure you, you would have frightened me too, if I had not known you to be an Ass."

The Fox and the Ape

Upon the decease of the Lion, the beasts of the forest assembled to choose another king. The Ape played so many grimaces, gambols, and antic tricks, that he was elected by a large majority; and the crown was placed upon his head. The Fox, envious of this distinction, seeing, soon after, a trap baited with a piece of meat, approached the new king, and said with mock humility: "May it please your majesty, I have found on your domain a treasure, to which, if you will deign to accompany me, I will conduct you." The Ape thereupon set off with the Fox, and, on arriving at the spot, laid his paw upon the meat. Snap! went the trap, and caught him by the fingers. Mad with the shame and the pain, he reproached the Fox for a false thief and a traitor. Reynard laughed heartily, and said, with a sneer: "

You a king, and not understand a trap!"

The Lion and the Wolf

A Wolf, roaming by the mountain's side, saw his own shadow, as the sun was setting, become greatly extended and magnified, and he said to himself: "Why should I, being of such an immense size, and extending nearly an acre in length, be afraid of the Lion? Ought I not to be acknowledged as King of all the collected beasts?" While he was indulging in these proud thoughts, a Lion fell upon him, and killed him. He exclaimed with a too-late repentance, "Wretched me! this over-estimation of myself is the cause of my destruction."

It is not wise, to hold too exalted an opinion of one's self.

The Miller, his Son and their Ass

A miller and his Son were driving their Ass to a fair. On the way, they met a troop of girls. "Look there!" cried one of them, "did you ever see such fools, to be trudging along on foot when they might be riding?" The old Man, hearing this, quietly bade his Son get on the Ass, and walked along merrily by his side.

Presently they came to a group of old men in earnest debate. "There!" said one of them, "it proves what I was saying. What respect is shown to old age in these days? Do you see that idle young rogue riding, while his old father has to walk?—Get down, you scapegrace! and let the old Man rest his weary limbs." Upon this the Father made his Son dismount, and got up himself. In this manner they had not proceeded far when they met a company of women and children. "Why, you lazy old fellow!" cried several tongues at once, "how can you ride upon the beast, while that poor little lad there can hardly keep pace by the side of you." The good-natured Miller immediately took up his Son behind him. They had now almost reached the town. "Pray, honest friend," said a townsman, "is that Ass your own?" "Yes," says the old Man. "Oh! One would not have thought so by the way you load him. Why, you two fellows are better able to carry the poor beast than he you!" "Anything to please you," said the old Man. So, alighting with his Son, they tied the Ass's legs together, and by the help of a pole endeavored to carry him on their shoulders over a bridge. The people ran out in crowds to laugh at the sight; till the Ass, not liking the noise nor his situation, kicked asunder the cords and, tumbling off the pole, fell into the river. Upon this the old Man made the best of his way home with his Son—convinced that, by endeavoring to please every-body, he had succeeded in pleasing nobody, and lost his Ass into the bargain.

The Travelers and the Plane-Tree

Two Travelers, worn out by the heat of the summer's sun, laid themselves down at noon under the wide-spreading branches of a Plane-tree. As they rested under its shade, one of the Travelers said to the other: "What a singularly useless tree is the Plane. It bears no fruit, and is not of the least service to man." The Plane-tree interrupting him said: "You ungrateful fellows! Do you, while receiving benefits from me, and resting under my shade, dare to describe me as useless, and unprofitable?"

Some men despise their best blessings because they come without cost.

The Tortoise and the Two Ducks

A Tortoise, becoming tired of her humble home, resolved to visit foreign lands, but she did not know which way to go. She repaired to two Ducks to show her the road, and they told her that the best way to travel was through the air. On her imploring their help, they made her grasp a stick with her mouth, and so they bore her aloft. As they flew along, the gaping people beneath shouted at sight of the spectacle. The vain Tortoise mistook their shouts for applause. "I am surely a queen," said she. But, alas! as she opened her mouth to speak she lost her hold of the stick, and, falling to the ground, was dashed to pieces.

Those who are not able to roam should stay at home.

The Madman who Sold Wisdom

A Madman once set himself up in the market place, and with loud cries announced that he would sell Wisdom. The people at once crowded about him, and some gave him gold for his wares, but they each got only a blow on the ear and a bunch of thread, and were well laughed at by their companions. One of them, however, took it more seriously than the others, and asked a wise sage what it meant. "It means," said the sage, "that if one would not be hurt by a Madman, he must put a bunch of thread over his ears."

So the Madman was really selling Wisdom.

The Countryman and the Snake

A Villager found a Snake under a hedge, almost dead with cold. He could not help having a compassion for the poor creature, so he brought it home, and laid it upon the hearth near the fire; but it had not lain there long, before (being revived with the heat) it began to erect itself, and fly at his wife and children. The Countryman, hearing an outcry, and perceiving what the matter was, caught up a mattock, and soon dispatched him, upbraiding him at the same time in these words: "Is this, vile wretch, the reward you make to him that saved your life?"

Kindness to the ungrateful and the vicious is thrown away.

The Leopard and the Fox

A Leopard, being no longer able, by reason of old age, to pursue his prey, feigned illness, and gave out that he would confer great favors upon any animal that would cure him. A cunning Fox heard of the proclamation, and lost no time in visiting the Leopard, first making himself look as much like a physician as he could. On seeing him, the Leopard declared that such a distinguished looking animal could not fail to cure him. This

so flattered the Fox that he came near, and at once fell a victim to his vanity, being unable to flee because of the disguise, which fettered his limbs.

Flattery is a dangerous weapon in the hands of an enemy.

The Hare afraid of his Ears

The Lion, being badly hurt by the horns of a goat, swore in a great rage that every animal with horns should be banished from his kingdom. A silly Hare, seeing the shadow of his ears, was in great fear lest they should be taken for horns, and scampered away.

The Peacock and the Crane

A Peacock, spreading its gorgeous tail, mocked a Crane that passed by, ridiculing the ashen hue of its plumage, and saying: "I am robed like a king, in gold and purple, and all the colors of the rainbow; while you have not a bit of color on your wings." "True," replied the Crane, "but I soar to the heights of heaven, and lift up my voice to the stars, while you walk below, like a cock, among the birds of the

dunghill."

Fine feathers don't make fine birds.

The Mouse and the Weasel

A little starveling Mouse had made his way with some difficulty into a basket of corn, where, finding the entertainment so good, he stuffed and crammed himself to such an extent, that when he would have got out again he found the hole was too small to allow his puffed-up body to pass. As he sat at the hole groaning over his fate, a Weasel, who was brought to the spot by his cries, thus addressed him: "Stop there, my friend, and fast till you are thin; for you will never come out till you reduce yourself to the same condition as when you entered."

The Fox and the Tiger

A skillful archer, coming into the woods, directed his arrows so successfully that he slew many wild beasts, and pursued several others. This put the whole savage kind into a fearful consternation, and made them fly to the most retired thickets for refuge. At last, the Tiger resumed courage, and, bidding them not be afraid, said that he alone would engage the enemy; telling them they might depend upon his valor and strength to revenge their wrongs. In the midst of these threats, while he was lashing himself with his tail, and tearing up the ground for anger, an arrow pierced his ribs, and hung by its barbed point in his side. He set up an hideous and loud roar, occasioned by the anguish which he felt, and endeavored to draw out the painful dart with his teeth; when the Fox, approaching him, inquired with an air of surprise who it was that could have strength and courage enough to wound so mighty and valorous a beast! "Ah!" says the Tiger, "I was mistaken in my reckoning: it was that invincible man yonder."

There is always some vulnerable point in the strongest armor.

The Fox and the Turkeys

A Fox spied some turkeys roosting in a tree. He managed to attract their attention and then ran about the tree, pretended to climb, walked on his hind legs, and did all sorts of tricks. Filled with fear, the Turkeys watched every one of his movements until they became dizzy, and, one by one, fell from their safe perch.

By too much attention to danger, we may fall victims to it.

The Eagle, the Cat, and the Wild Sow

An Eagle had made her nest at the top of a lofty oak. A Cat, having found a convenient hole, lived with her kittens in the middle of the trunk; and a Wild Sow with her young had taken shelter in a hollow at its foot. The Cat resolved to destroy by her arts this chance-made colony. She climbed to the nest of the Eagle, and said: "Destruction is preparing for you, and for me

too. The Wild Sow, whom you may see daily digging up the earth, wishes to uproot the oak, that she may, on its fall, seize our families as food." Then she crept down to the cave of the Sow and said: "Your children are in great danger; for as soon as you shall go out with your litter to find food, the Eagle is prepared to pounce upon one of your little pigs." When night came, she went forth with silent foot and obtained food for herself and her kittens; but, feigning to be afraid, she kept a look-out all through the day. Meanwhile, the Eagle, full of fear of the Sow, sat still on the branches, and the Sow, terrified by the Eagle, did not dare to go out from her cave; and thus they each, with their families, perished from hunger.

Those who stir up enmities are not to be trusted.

The Peacock and the Magpie

The Birds once met together to choose a king; and, among others, the Peacock was a candidate. Spreading his showy tail, and stalking up and down with affected grandeur, he caught the eyes of the silly multitude by his brilliant appearance, and was elected with acclamation. The Magpie then stepped forth into the midst of the assembly, and thus addressed the new king: "May it please your majesty, elect to permit a humble admirer to propose a question. As our king, we put our lives and fortunes in your hands. If, therefore, the Eagle, the Vulture, and the Kite, should make a descent upon us, what means would you take for our defense?" This pithy question opened the eyes of the Birds to the weakness of their choice and they canceled the election.

The Man Bitten by a Dog

A Man who had been bitten by a Dog was going about asking who could cure him. One that met him said: "Sir, if you would be cured, take a bit of bread and dip it in the blood of the wound, and give it to the dog that bit you." The Man smiled, and said: "If I were to follow your advice, I should be bitten by all the dogs in the city."

He who proclaims himself ready to buy up his enemies will never want a supply of them.

The Two Goats

Two Goats started at the same moment, from opposite ends, to cross a rude bridge that was only wide enough for one to cross at a time. Meeting at the middle of the bridge, neither would give way to the other. They locked horns and fought for the right of way, until they both fell into the torrent below and were drowned.

The Dove and the Ant

An Ant went to the bank of a river to quench its thirst, and, being carried away by the rush of the stream, was on the point of being drowned. A Dove, sitting on a tree overhanging the water, plucked a leaf, and let it fall into the stream close to her. The Ant, climbing on to it, floated in safety to the bank. Shortly afterwards a bird catcher came close and stood under the tree, and laid his lime-twigs for the Dove, which sat in the branches. The Ant, perceiving his  design, stung him in the foot. He suddenly threw down the twigs, and thereupon made the Dove take wing.

The grateful heart will always find opportunities to show its gratitude.

The Eagle and the Beetle

The Eagle and the Beetle were at enmity together, and they destroyed one another's nests. The Eagle gave the first provocation in seizing upon and in eating the young ones of the Beetle. The Beetle got by stealth at the Eagle's eggs, and rolled them out of the nest, and followed the Eagle even into the presence of Jupiter. On the Eagle making his complaint, Jupiter ordered him to make his nest in his lap; and while Jupiter had the eggs in his lap, the Beetle came flying about him, and Jupiter, rising up unawares to drive him away from his head, threw down the eggs, and broke them.

The weak often revenge themselves on those who use them ill, even though they be the more powerful.

The Mule

A Mule, frolicsome from want of work and from overmuch corn, galloped about in a very extravagant manner, and said to himself: "My father surely was a high-mettled racer, and I am his own child in speed and spirit." On the next day, being driven a long journey, and feeling very weary, he exclaimed in a disconsolate tone: "I must have made a mistake; my father, after all, could have been only an ass."

The Cat, the Weasel and the Rabbit

While a Rabbit was absent from his hole one day, a Weasel took possession of it. On the Rabbit's return, seeing the Weasel's nose sticking out, he said: "You must leave this hole immediately. There is only room for one, and it has always belonged to me and my fathers before me." "The more reason that you should give it up now," said the Weasel, "and leave its possession to me." As they could not settle the dispute, they agreed to leave the question of ownership to a wise old Cat, to whom they went without more ado. "I am deaf," said the Cat. "Put your noses close to my ears." No sooner had they done so, than she clapped a paw upon each of them, and killed them both.

The strong are apt to settle all questions by the rule of might.

The Widow and the Sheep

There was a certain Widow who had an only Sheep, and, wishing to make the most of his wool, she sheared him so closely that she cut his skin as well as his fleece. The Sheep, smarting under this treatment, cried out: "Why do you torture me thus? What will my blood add to the weight of the wool? If you want my flesh, Dame, send for the Butcher, who will put me out of my misery at once; but if you want my fleece, send for the Shearer, who will clip my wool without drawing my blood."

Economy may be carried too far.

The Rat and the Frog

A Rat in an evil day made acquaintance with a Frog, and they set off on their travels together. The Frog, on pretense of great affection, and of keeping his companion out of harm's way, tied the Rat's foot to his own hind-leg, and thus they proceeded for some distance by land. Presently they came to some water, and the Frog, bidding the Rat have good courage, began to swim across. They had scarcely, however, arrived midway, when the Frog took a sudden plunge to the bottom, dragging the unfortunate Rat after him. But the struggling and floundering of the Rat made so great a commotion in the water that it attracted the attention of a Kite, who, pouncing down and bearing off the Rat, carried away the Frog at the same time in his train.

Inconsiderate and ill-matched alliances generally end in ruin; and the man who compasses the destruction of his neighbor, is often caught in his own snare.

The Goatherd and the Goats

It was a stormy day, and the snow was falling fast, when a Goatherd drove his Goats, all white with snow, into a desert cave for shelter. There he found that a herd of Wild Goats, more numerous and larger than his own, had already taken possession. So, thinking to secure them all, he left his own Goats to take care of themselves, and threw the branches which he had brought for them to the Wild Goats to browse on. But when the weather cleared up, he found his own Goats had perished from hunger, while the Wild Goats were off and away to the hills and woods. So the Goatherd returned a laughing-stock to his neighbors, having failed to gain the Wild Goats, and having lost his own.

They who neglect their old friends for the sake of new ones, are rightly served if they lose both.

The Horse and the Wolf

A Wolf saw a Horse grazing in a field. Putting on a grave air, he approached him and said: "Sir, you must be very ill; I have some skill as a physician, and if you will tell me where your ailment is, I shall be glad to be of service." Said the horse: "If you will examine my foot, you will find what ails me." But as the wily Wolf approached him, with a kick he sent him flying into the air.

The Goose with the Golden Eggs

A certain man had the good fortune to possess a Goose that laid him a Golden Egg every day. But dissatisfied with so slow an income, and thinking to seize the whole treasure at once, he killed the Goose, and cutting her open, found her—just what any other goose would be!

Much wants more, and loses all.

124

The Old Woman and the Wine-Jar

An Old Woman found an empty jar which had lately been full of prime old wine, and which still retained the fragrant smell of its former contents. She greedily placed it several times to her nose, and drawing it backwards and forwards, said: "O most delicious! How nice must the Wine itself have been when it leaves behind in the very vessel which contained it so sweet a perfume!"

The memory of a good deed lives.

The Ass Carrying Salt

A certain Huckster who kept an Ass, hearing that Salt was to be had cheap at the sea-side, drove down his Ass thither to buy some. Having loaded the beast as much as he could bear, he was driving him home, when, as they were passing a slippery ledge of rock, the Ass fell into the stream below, and the Salt being melted, the Ass

was relieved of his burden, and having gained the bank with ease, pursued his journey onward, light in body and in spirit. The Huckster soon afterwards set off for the sea-shore for some more Salt, and loaded the Ass, if possible, yet more heavily than before. On their return, as they crossed the stream into which he had formerly fallen, the Ass fell down on purpose, and by the dissolving of the Salt, was again released from his load. The Master, provoked at the loss, and thinking how he might cure him of this trick, on his next journey to the coast freighted the beast with a load of sponges. When they arrived at the same stream as before, the Ass was at his old tricks again, and rolled himself into the water; but he found to his cost, as he proceeded homewards, that instead of lightening his burden, he had more than doubled its weight.

The same measures will not suit all circumstances.

The Gnat and the Bull

A Gnat that had been buzzing about the head of a Bull, at length settling himself down upon his horn, begged his pardon for incommoding him; "but if," says he, "my weight at all inconveniences you, pray say so, and I will be off in a moment." "Oh, never trouble your head about that," says the Bull, "for 'tis all one to me whether you go or stay; and, to say the truth, I did not know you were there."

The smaller the Mind the greater the Conceit.

The Lion and the Gnat

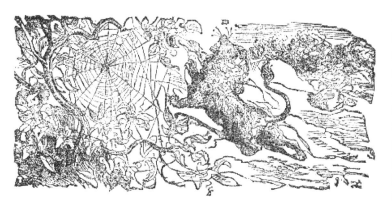

As a Gnat was buzzing around a Lion, the Lion said to him: "How dare you approach so near? Be off, or I will kill you with the least stroke of my paw." The Gnat, knowing the advantage of his small size, and his alertness, immediately challenged the boaster to combat, and alighting first upon his nose and then upon his tail, made the Lion so furious that he injured himself grievously with his paws. As the Gnat flew away he boasted of his own prowess in thus defeating the King of Beasts without the slightest injury to himself. But, in his carelessness, he flew directly into a spider's web, and the spider instantly seized and killed him.

The Lion, the Ass and the Fox Hunting

The Lion, the Ass and the Fox formed a party to go out hunting. They took a large booty, and when the sport was ended, bethought themselves of having a hearty meal. The Lion bade the Ass allot the spoil. So, dividing it into three equal parts, the Ass begged his friends to make their choice; at which the Lion, in great indignation, fell upon the Ass and tore him to pieces. He then bade the Fox make a division; who, gathering the whole into one great heap, reserved but the smallest mite for himself. "Ah! friend," says the Lion, "who taught you to make so equitable a division?" "I wanted no other lesson," replied the Fox, "than the Ass's fate."

Better be wise by the misfortunes of others than by your own.

The Dog Whose Ears were Cropped

A Dog complained of the cruelty of her master in cutting off her ears, and was so ashamed of her appearance that she resolved to stay in her kennel with her family. A friendly hunting dog said to her: "If you had been peaceful, and not always fighting, you would have saved your ears and your good looks. If you will fight, it is a kindness to crop your ears, that they may not give your enemy the advantage."

The Wild Boar and the Fox

A Wild Boar was whetting his tusks against a tree, when a Fox coming by, asked why he did so; "for," said he, "I see no reason for it; there is neither hunter nor hound in sight, nor any other danger that I can see, at hand." "True," replied the Boar; "but when that danger does arise, I shall have something else to do than to sharpen my weapons."

It is too late to whet the sword when the trumpet sounds to draw it.

The Wind and the Sun

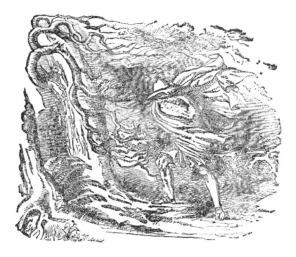

A dispute once arose between the Wind and the Sun, which was the stronger of the two, and they agreed to settle the point upon this issue—that whichever of the two soonest made a traveler take off his cloak, should be accounted the more powerful. The Wind began, and blew with all his might and main a blast, cold and fierce as a Thracian storm; but the stronger he blew, the closer the traveler wrapped his cloak around him, and the tighter he grasped it with his hands. Then broke out the Sun. With his welcome beams he dispersed the vapor and the cold; the traveler felt the genial warmth, and as the Sun shone brighter and brighter, he sat down, quite overcome with the heat, and taking off his cloak, cast it on the ground.

Thus the Sun was declared the conqueror; and it has ever been deemed that persuasion is better than force; and that the sunshine of a kind and gentle manner will sooner lay open a poor man's heart than all the threatenings and force of blustering authority.

The Hunter and the Wolf

A greedy Hunter one day shot a fine Deer, and ere he could dress it, a pretty Fawn came that way, and an arrow brought it to the ground. A Boar now chanced to be passing, and the Hunter wounded it so that it lay upon the ground as if dead. Not satisfied with this game, he must needs pursue a Partridge that came fluttering near, and

while he was doing so the wounded Boar regained enough strength to spring upon him and kill him. A Wolf came that way, and seeing the four dead bodies, said: "Here is food for a month; but I will save the best, and be content to-day with the bow-string." But when he seized the string it loosened the fixed arrow, which shot him through the heart.

The greedy man and the miser cannot enjoy their gains.

The Astronomer

An Astronomer used to walk out every night to gaze upon the stars. It happened one night that, with his whole thoughts rapt up in the skies, he fell into a well. One who heard his cries ran up to him, and said: "While you are trying to pry into the mysteries of heaven, you overlook the common objects under your feet."

We should never look so high as to miss seeing the things that are around us.

The Bulls and the Frogs

Two Bulls lived in the same herd, and each aspiring to be the leader and master, they finally engaged in a fierce battle. An old Frog, who sat on the bank of a stream near by, began to groan and to quake with fear. A thoughtless young Frog said to the old one: "Why need you be afraid? What is it to you that the Bulls fight for supremacy?" "Do you not see," said the old Frog, "that one must defeat the other, and that the defeated Bull, being driven from the field, will be forced to stay in the marshes, and will thus trample us to death?"

The poor and weak are often made to suffer for the follies of the great.

The Thief and His Mother

A Schoolboy stole a horn-book from one of his schoolfellows, and brought it home to his mother. Instead of chastising him, she rather encouraged him in the deed. In course of time the boy, now grown into a man, began to steal things of greater value, until, at last, being caught in the very act, he was brought to the Judge and sentenced to be hung. As he was being led to the scaffold, the mother bowed herself to the ground with grief. A neighbor seeing her thus, said to her: "It is too late for you to moan and sob now. If you had been as much grieved when he committed his first theft, you would have corrected him in time, and thus have saved yourself this sorrowful day."

Nip evil in the bud.

The Man and His Two Wives

In days when a man was allowed more wives than one, a middle-aged bachelor, who could be called neither young nor old, and whose hair was only just beginning to turn gray, must needs fall in love with two women at once, and marry them both. The one was young and blooming, and wished her husband to appear as youthful as herself; the other was somewhat more advanced in age, and was as anxious that her husband should appear a suitable match for her. So, while the young one seized every opportunity of pulling out the good man's gray hairs, the old one was as industrious in plucking out every black hair she could find, till he found that, between the one and the other, he had not a hair left.

He that submits his principles to the influence and caprices of opposite parties will end in having no principles at all.

The Heifer, the Goat, the Sheep and the Lion

A Heifer, a Goat, a Sheep, and a Lion formed a partnership, and agreed to divide their earnings. The Goat having snared a stag, they sent for the Lion to divide it for them. The Lion said: "I will make four parts—the first shall be mine as judge; the second, because I am strongest; the third, because I am bravest; and the fourth—I will kill any one who dares touch it."

He who will steal a part will steal the whole.

The Camel and the Travelers

Two Travelers on a desert saw a Camel in the distance, and were greatly frightened at his huge appearance, thinking it to be some huge monster. While they hid behind some low shrubs, the animal came nearer, and they discovered that it was only a harmless Camel which had excited their fears.

Distance exaggerates dangers.

The Swan and the Goose

A certain rich man bought in the market a Goose and a Swan. He fed the one for his table, and kept the other for the sake of its song. When the time came for killing the Goose, the cook went to take him at night, when it was dark, and he was not able to distinguish one bird from the other, and he caught the Swan instead of the Goose. The Swan, threatened with death, burst forth into song, and thus made himself known by his voice, and preserved his life by his melody.

Sweet words may deliver us from peril, when harsh words would fail.

The Dolphins and the Sprat

The Dolphins and the Whales were at war with one another, and the Sprat stepped in and endeavored to separate them. But one of the Dolphins cried out: "We would rather perish in the contest, than be reconciled by you."

The Shepherd and the Sea

A Shepherd moved down his flock to feed near the shore, and beholding the Sea lying in a smooth calm, he was seized with a strong desire to sail over it. So he sold all his sheep and bought a cargo of Dates, and loaded a vessel, and set sail. He had not gone far when a storm arose; his ship was wrecked, and his Dates

and everything lost, and he himself with difficulty escaped to land. Not long after, when the

Sea was again calm, and one of his friends came up to him and was admiring its repose, he said: "Have a care, my good fellow, of that smooth surface, it is only looking out for your Dates."

The Bees, the Drones, and the Wasp

Some Bees had built their comb in the hollow trunk of an oak. The Drones asserted that it was their doing, and belonged to them. The cause was brought into court before Judge Wasp. Knowing something of the parties, he thus addressed them: "The plaintiffs and defendants are so much alike in shape and color as to render the ownership a doubtful matter. Let each party take a hive to itself, and build up a new comb, that from the shape of the cells and the taste of the honey, the lawful proprietors of the property in dispute may appear." The Bees readily assented to the Wasp's plan. The Drones declined it. Whereupon the Wasp gave judgment: "It is clear now who made the comb, and who cannot make it; the Court adjudges the honey to the Bees."

Professions are best tested by deeds.

The Wolf, the Goat and the Kid

As an old Goat was going forth to pasture, she carefully latched her door, and bid her kid not to open it to any one who could not give this pass-word: "Beware of the Wolf and all his race." A Wolf happened to be passing, and overheard what the old Goat said. When she was gone, he went to the door, and, knocking, said: "Beware of the Wolf and all his race." But the Kid, peeping through a crack, said: "Show me a white paw and I will open the door." As the Wolf could not do this, he had to depart, no better than he came.

Two sureties are better than one.

The Fox and the Hedgehog

A Fox, while crossing over a river, was driven by the stream into a narrow gorge, and lay there for a long time unable to get out, covered with myriads of horse-flies that had fastened themselves upon him. A Hedgehog, who was wandering in that direction, saw him, and taking compassion on him, asked him if he should drive away the flies that were so tormenting him. But the Fox begged him to do nothing of the sort. "Why not?" asked the Hedgehog. "Because," replied the Fox, "these flies that are upon me now are already full, and draw but little blood, but should you remove them, a swarm of fresh and hungry ones will come, who will not leave a drop of blood in my body."

When we throw off rulers or dependents, who have already made the most of us, we do but, for the most part, lay ourselves open to others, who will make us bleed yet more freely.

The Brazier and His Dog

A Brazier had a little Dog, which was a great favorite with his master, and his constant companion. While he hammered away at his metals the Dog slept; but when, on the other hand, he went to dinner, and began to eat, the Dog woke up, and wagged his tail, as if he would ask for a share of his meal. His master one day, pretending to be angry, and shaking his stick at him, said: "You wretched little sluggard! what shall I do to you? While I am hammering on the anvil, you sleep on the mat, and when I begin to eat after my toil, you wake up and wag your tail for food.

Do you not know that labor is the source of every blessing, and that none but those who work are entitled to eat?"

The Wild Ass and the Lion

A Wild Ass and a Lion entered into an alliance that they might capture the beasts of the forest with the greater ease. The Lion agreed to assist the Wild Ass with strength, while the Wild Ass gave the Lion the benefit of his greater speed. When they had taken as many beasts as their necessities required, the Lion undertook to distribute the prey, and for this purpose divided it into three shares. "I will take the first share," he said, "because I am king; and the second share, as a partner with you in the chase; and the third share (believe me) will be a source of great evil to you, unless you willingly resign it to me, and set off as fast as you can."

Might makes right.

The Father and His Two Daughters

A man had two daughters, the one married to a gardener, and the other to a tile-maker. After a time he went to the daughter who had married the gardener, and inquired how she was, and how all things went with her. She said: "All things are prospering with me, and I have only one wish, that there may be a heavy fall of rain, in order that the plants may be well watered." Not long after he went to the daughter who had married the tile-maker, and likewise inquired of her how she fared; she replied: "I want for nothing, and have only one wish, that the dry weather may continue, and the sun shine hot and bright, so that the bricks might be dried." He said to her: "If your sister wishes for rain, and you for dry weather, with which of the two am I to join my wishes?"

The Fir Tree and the Bramble

A Fir Tree said boastingly to the Bramble: "You are useful for nothing at all, while I am everywhere used for roofs and houses." The Bramble made answer: "You poor creature, if you would only call to mind the axes and saws which are about to hew you down, you would have reason to wish that you had grown up a Bramble, not a Fir Tree."

Better poverty without care, than riches with.

The Fox and the Monkey

A Monkey once danced in an assembly of the Beasts, and so pleased them all by his performance that they elected him their king. A Fox envying him the honor, discovered a piece of meat lying in a trap, and leading the Monkey to the place where it was, said "that she had found a store, but had not used it, but had kept it for him as treasure trove of his kingdom, and counseled him to lay hold of it." The Monkey approached carelessly, and was caught in the trap; and on his accusing the Fox of purposely leading him into the snare, she replied: "O Monkey, and are you, with such a mind as yours, going to be king over the Beasts?"

The Farmer and His Sons

A Farmer being on the point of death, wished to insure from his sons the same attention to his farm as he had himself given it. He called them to his bedside, and said: "My sons, there is a great treasure hid in one of my vineyards." The sons, after his death, took their spades and mattocks, and carefully dug over every portion of their land. They found no treasure, but the vines repaid their labor by an extraordinary and superabundant crop.

The Cat and the Birds

A Cat, hearing that the Birds in a certain aviary were ailing, dressed himself up as a physician, and, taking with him his cane and the instruments becoming his profession, went to the aviary, knocked at the door, and inquired of the inmates how they all did, saying that if they were ill, he would be happy to prescribe for them and cure them. They replied: "We are all very well, and shall continue so, if you will only be good enough to go away, and leave us as we are."

The Stag, the Wolf and the Sheep

A Stag asked a Sheep to lend him a measure of wheat, and said that the Wolf would be his surety. The Sheep, fearing some fraud was intended, excused herself, saying: "The Wolf is accustomed to seize what he wants, and to run off, and you, too, can quickly out-strip me in your rapid flight. How then shall I be able to find you when the day of payment comes?"

Two blacks do not make one white.

The Raven and the Swan

A Raven saw a Swan, and desired to secure for himself a like beauty of plumage. Supposing that his splendid white color arose from his washing in the water in which he swam, the Raven left the altars in the neighborhood of which he picked up his living, and took up his abode in the lakes and pools. But cleansing his feathers as often as he would, he could not change their color, while through want of food he perished.

Change of habit cannot alter nature.

The Lioness

A controversy prevailed among the beasts of the field, as to which of the animals deserved the most credit for producing the greatest number of whelps at a birth. They rushed clamorously into the presence of the Lioness, and demanded of her the settlement of the dispute. "And you," they said, "how many sons have you at a birth?" The Lioness laughed at them, and said: "Why! I have only one; but that one is altogether a thorough-bred Lion."

The value is in the worth, not in the number.

Aesop's Fables (Illustrated)

Aesop's Fables (Illustrated)

Made in the USA
Las Vegas, NV
15 March 2021

19600173R00077